The
Message
of the
Mask

by
Elfreida Read

cover and illustrations
by
Sharin Barber

gage PUBLISHING LIMITED
TORONTO ONTARIO CANADA

The Message of the Mask is an adaptation of a book previously published under the title *Twin Rivers* by Burns & MacEachern Limited.

ISBN 0-7715-6298-5

3 4 5 6 7 8 9 WC 86 85 84

Contents

Chapter 1

A Birthday

What would it be? Scott wriggled under his blankets, trying to guess.

Perhaps it would be a rare rock for his collection, from Africa or South America, but then Jake didn't believe in buying rocks. Jake thought you should go out and find them for yourself.

Could it be a new fishing-line? Or some paints? Scott had seen some oil paints in a store the other day. He had always wanted oil paints, but maybe they were too expensive. Perhaps it would be something dull, like a shirt, or socks. That wouldn't be like Jake, though. In all the six years that Scott had lived with Jake O'Burn, Jake had never given him anything useful and boring for his birthday.

Scott recalled his past two birthdays. At ten, his sweater had been torn, but Jake had given him ice skates! At eleven, he'd really needed a new pair of shoes — but Jake had given him a knife with six blades and a splendid rock-pick! Somehow the sweater and the shoes had also appeared in due time, but Jake didn't consider such things suitable birthday gifts.

Scott turned over, and his bed creaked. The moon was shining right into his window, and the waving shadow of the giant pine just outside performed a slow and graceful dance upon the walls of his little room. Scott could smell the forest. He loved that special fragrance of the pines especially at night; it made him feel safe and at home.

What would his present be tomorrow? Scott wondered again.

He wriggled a toe through a hole in the bottom of his sheet. His toe got stuck, so he sat up to free it. He peered at his clock. It was only eleven. Eight hours to go. And he was still wide awake.

Scott's thoughts went from his birthday to Jake. The older he became, the more he realized how lucky he was to have had Jake when his parents died. Jake had been his father's best friend, and when Scott's parents were killed in a car crash it just seemed natural for Jake to take care of him. Scott's parents had no other relatives, and Jake had always been good to him. He'd played with Scott and brought him little gifts even when it wasn't Christmas or his birthday.

Scott had been six years old when Jake brought him to Twin Rivers, the tiny motel set on the slopes above the Fraser Canyon, close to where the Thompson River met the Fraser. How kind and patient Jake had been and how understanding of a small boy's grief and loneliness. When Scott thought of Jake like this, in the middle of the dark, quiet night, he got a funny feeling in his throat, and a warm feeling inside.

How he wished he could fall asleep. . . .

Suddenly the sun was flooding the tiny bedroom. Scott blinked his eyes. So he had fallen asleep after all, and the great day was here!

Scott's clock told him that it was still very early, too early to waken Jake. He lay in bed impatiently, watching the first rays of the sun light up the whitewashed walls of his room and highlight the paintings he had pinned up on them, the ones that had come out the best. There weren't many. Most of them were hidden away with his other stuff in a box under his bed.

Slowly the sunlight reached the bureau in the corner, picking out the little wooden figures over which Scott had labored on many winter evenings when there was nothing much else to do in the snow-bound motel. He had painted some of those too. Jake said that if he kept at it, someone might buy some of his work one day. But Scott didn't know if he would ever want to sell what he had made.

It *had* to be time to get up by now, and even if it *wasn't*, Scott was going to get up anyway. He climbed out of bed and peered down the narrow hall. There was still no sound coming from Jake's room. Scott opened the front door and stepped out. Nobody else was up. The little cottages of Jake's motel were bathed in the slanted light of sunrise. A robin screamed by Scott's head. The robins had a nest in the eaves and both the parent birds were very protective of their family.

Flappy appeared and jumped up at Scott with a little yelp. Scott sat down on the doorstep, with Flappy in his lap, and fondled his dog's big ears.

"Oh ho, oh ho!" Jake's voice suddenly boomed behind him. "Up with the robins this morning, eh? Happy birthday, kid."

Scott leapt to his feet, displacing Flappy who barked in protest.

"How's the birthday boy?" Jake asked, giving Flappy a friendly slap and putting an arm around Scott.

9

"Fine," Scott said. His eyes shone with expectation.

Jake grinned back at him. "Come on then," he said, "there might be something of interest on that breakfast table this morning."

Scott followed Jake into the kitchen. Eagerly he scanned the breakfast table, but there was no parcel by his plate, nor was there anything on his chair or on the floor by the table. In fact there was nothing at all anywhere, except the traditional envelope, with the birthday card in it, on his plate.

Scott felt a faint twinge of anxiety. He knew that Jake did not make very much money out of his motel, and he knew that some of the money went to an invalid sister in Regina. Perhaps this time Jake had simply been unable to afford a present. Perhaps the explanation was in the card. But Scott wasn't given much time for thought.

"Come on, come on," Jake urged him.

Puzzled, Scott sat down quickly at the table and tore open the birthday-card envelope. He pulled the card out, grinned at the funny picture on the front, and then opened it.

And there it was, his gift.

"Oh, Jake!" Scott's voice had a funny crack in it. "Railway tickets!" Not even in his wildest imaginings would Scott have considered this as a possibility. "Jake! Where are we going?"

"The coast," Jake replied. "Vancouver. We'll explore everything—Vancouver Island, Victoria, Long Beach, you name it."

"But Jake," Scott's voice was still a little hoarse, "how can we afford a trip? Two of the cottages are empty. Oh, Jake, are you sure?"

"A birthday's a birthday, I always say," Jake replied. "Would you have preferred a set of underwear?"

Scott pushed his chair aside and gave Jake a great hug. His face brushed up against Jake's cheek. It felt like rough sandpaper.

"There's nothing, just nothing I'd rather have," he cried. "I'll really see all the places they tell us about in school! I just never thought we could afford anything like this."

"Well, we can't afford it, but we're going anyway," Jake said. "It won't be as expensive as it seems because we're going to stay with Sandy Black in Vancouver, and he wants to show us all the sights. Jeremiah will look after this place till we get back, and Annie will help him."

Jeremiah seemed as old as the forests. Nobody knew where he came from, and he couldn't remember himself. One spring day, many years ago, he had appeared at Twin Rivers and stayed. He helped Jake, and the visitors liked him, for he never ran out of tales of the Old West, of the goldrush days, of the wagon trails, the Indians, and the first settlers. "Annie" was Annie McKay. She was a Salish and the grandmother of Scott's best friend, Daniel.

"Sandy used to pass by a lot with his truck but he doesn't any more, does he?" Scott said. "Not since he got to be a partner in that big company."

"That's right. It was a good deal. He's made a lot of money, and he says he's had free meals here so often during his truck-driving days that it's time for him to play host."

"Is he your very best friend?"

"As good a friend as a man can have. He says he'll show us everything. You'll see the ocean, Scottyboy!"

Scott had never seen the ocean. Once he had been to a movie that had shown the breakers roaring on the Pacific Coast, and it had filled him with a bursting feeling

11

which had ballooned inside him and then settled down like a pain, somewhere in his middle.

He had had that same feeling when he had seen the prairies for the first time. On one of his truck runs, Sandy Black had taken Jake and Scott to see Jake's invalid sister in Regina. During the whole trip, Scott could scarcely speak. He felt that he was drowning in the soft, bright yellow ocean of wheat. He couldn't get enough of that rippling, gleaming world.

"Canada," Sandy had said simply, as though that explained everything. And when they had driven through the towering peaks in the heart of the Rockies, Sandy had said "Canada" again. Sometimes Scott had a fancy that his heart was shaped like the map of Canada. The parts he knew were brightly illumined, the other parts dark and exciting, waiting for him to get to know them. The whole map felt very warm and close, deep inside him.

"Oh, Jake!" Scott said again. "We're going to see the ocean. I can hardly wait to tell Dan." And, as soon as breakfast was over, he hurried to his friend's house.

Chapter 2

A Very Special Gift

Daniel and his grandmother lived in the woods beyond the motel and made a small living by helping Jake keep the motel neat and clean for visitors in the summer, and by selling the baskets and bags and mats that Mrs. McKay made in the winter. They belonged to the Thompson group of the Interior Salish Indians and Granny McKay, as everyone called her, followed the fine tradition of the Thompsons in her work. She was very skilful, and her work sold well.

Daniel and Scott went to school together in Lytton and spent their free hours exploring in the woods, collecting rocks, and swimming and fishing in the pools made by the river as it tumbled to the waiting sea.

Scott knocked impatiently at the door of his friend's house. "Dan," he called, "Dan!"

There was no immediate answer, but Scott heard the sound of hurried, muffled footsteps, a faint giggle, and Granny McKay's voice saying, "Be careful now." Then the door burst open and Daniel and his grandmother were saying, "Happy birthday, Scott. Happy

13

birthday!" Mrs. McKay was holding a cake, gaily decorated with candles, and Daniel had a parcel in his hands.

"Oh wow!" Scott exclaimed at the sight of the beautiful cake.

Granny McKay put the cake platter into Scott's hands, but she only let him hold it for a moment. "This cake is for our birthday supper with Jake," she said. "Do you like it?"

"Do I like it!" Scott managed to say. "It's gorgeous! Thank you, Granny."

Dan pressed his gift into Scott's hands. "Open my present, open it," he cried, jumping up and down.

The two boys sat down on the doorstep, and while Scott took the wrapping off Dan's large, rustly present, Daniel watched him eagerly. The wrapping came off and Scott gasped.

"Oh, Dan!" he exclaimed, awed. "It's fantastic! Where did you get it?"

Scott was holding a wooden mask in his hands, handsomely carved, beautifully painted.

"It's been in Gran's family for ages. There are two of them — twin masks. Come on in. I'll show you the other."

Excitedly, Daniel ran into the house, followed by Scott, and brought out another mask from a cupboard in the front room. It did indeed look like a perfect twin to Scott's gift. "I'm to have this one when I get to be twelve, but I've sort of got it already — unofficially," he laughed.

"What kind of masks are they?" Scott asked. "They're not the kind they used to wear around here, are they, Dan?"

"You mean those hooded 'tsewheys'? No. Those were made of grasses and bark and stuff like that. These came from far away. That's why they're special. When

14

the missionaries asked our people to get rid of the tsewheys, they did. But these masks were saved."

"How come?" Scott asked.

"They weren't tsewheys so they weren't used in our religious ceremonies. They're antiques now." He touched the masks with respect. "There's a story about them. Come on, Gran will tell you."

Granny McKay had placed the marvellous birthday cake on a safe shelf and was cleaning up the breakfast dishes. The boys joined her in the kitchen and helped.

"Gran," Dan said as they finished, "tell Scott about the masks."

Mrs. McKay sat down at the table. That's what was so nice about Granny McKay, she always made time for Daniel and Scott.

To the two boys, Granny McKay seemed very old. Actually she was in her late sixties. Her hair was a soft grey and she wore it pulled back from her face and twisted into a knot at the back of her head. Tiny lines crisscrossed her skin, which seemed fragile, like elegant tan-colored parchment. Although she always listened carefully to whatever the boys had to say, sometimes her dark eyes had a way of looking just a little beyond them, as though she were trying to draw something out of the past into the present for them to see. At such times, her eyes became dreamy and she would speak slowly.

Now that dreamy look came into Granny McKay's eyes. "The masks have been in my family for a very long time," she said. "No one really knows how long or where they came from. There was some connection with the Lillooets on my side of the family and they used to trade with the people on the coast, so they may have come from there."

"But the story," Dan urged, "the story, Gran."

16

"Yes, well, the story goes that two brothers in my family helped a strange shaman who was in trouble and he gave them these masks in return for their help."

"You know what a shaman is, don't you?" Dan said to Scott.

"Of course," Scott replied. "He's a wise man."

"And people believed they could do magic and all that. Go on, Gran."

"The shaman told them that they would always be able to keep in touch through these masks, no matter how far apart they were. Of course the people around here weren't used to masks like these and they were a bit afraid—everyone is a little uneasy with anything strange—but the brothers were sure that no harm could come of something given in goodwill." Granny thought for a moment and then went on:

"Now one of the brothers loved travelling, so he left the village and went to visit the people on the coast. They were kind to him, the climate was good, there was lots of food. He was enjoying himself and they wanted him to stay on with them. But one night, when they were having a feast, he put on his mask to do a dance . . ."

"And the mask spoke to him!" Dan said excitedly.

"He thought he heard the mask speaking to him," Granny said. "He had a feeling that the mask was telling him to go home. He was sure he had imagined it, but nonetheless he began to think about his home and how his place was really among his own people."

"And then the next day the same thing happened!" Dan again interrupted eagerly.

"So goes the story. Once again he had the strange feeling that the mask was trying to tell him something, and this time it was very strong. He felt he had to go home at once or it would be too late. He got very worried and went home as fast as he could. There was bad news." Granny McKay looked at the boys sadly. "His brother had gone on a hunting trip a few days before and had not returned. Scouts had been sent out to look for him but they had not found him. They said there was no hope of finding him alive."

"But he couldn't believe his brother was dead," Dan said.

"No, he couldn't. He was determined to try to find him himself. He went to look for him. He had no idea where to go. He wandered around in the woods trying to imagine where his brother might have gone."

"And then it happened again!" Dan was watching Scott's face. His eyes were large as he relived the drama in his own mind.

"He had that same strange feeling," Granny went on, "telling him where he should go. He followed the urge, and found his brother. He had been mauled by a bear and was close to death. But he was brought home and nursed back to health. And that's the way all good stories end, isn't it?" Granny smiled.

Scott smiled too, and nodded thoughtfully. He turned the mask over in his hands. It was certainly very old. But the carving was beautiful and the paint still intact. It was a real treasure.

"Isn't that a great story?" Dan said.

"It sure is," Scott agreed, "the best one I've ever heard." He ran a finger over the curved mouth of the mask. "I wonder if it *could* talk once upon a time..."

"Perhaps it's just an old tale to explain the masks," Granny McKay said. "But you know people do get these feelings."

She shook her head at the strangeness of life.

"Gran believes all kinds of things," Dan teased.

"Not all kinds of things," Granny McKay corrected him. "But some things, yes." She touched each of the masks gently with the tips of her fingers.

Watching her and seeing the look of wistfulness on her face, Scott felt sure that Granny did believe that some of that ancient magic still lingered in the masks. He himself certainly wanted to believe it. But then Granny straightened up, and her manner became matter-of-fact again.

"Now, enough of all this talk of magic masks," she said. "We've all got lots of work to do."

Scott and Dan wandered slowly out of the house and lingered by the doorway.

"How come you're giving me the mask?" Scott asked diffidently. "Shouldn't it stay in your family, Dan?"

"Granny and I are the only ones left in our family," Daniel said, "and now—since I've given one of the masks to you—it's like—you're my brother." He looked at Scott a little shyly.

"Thanks, Dan," Scott said a bit gruffly, keeping his eyes firmly on the mask. "I already feel like that—but this will make it kind of official." He was feeling that warm, bursting feeling again.

"It's good luck, too," Daniel said. "You have to take it with you wherever you go. You must never part with it, you know."

"Part with it!" Scott laughed. "I guess not. What an idea! It's the greatest thing I've ever had." He held the mask to himself, closely, but carefully.

"Say, what else did you get?" Dan asked. "What did Jake give you?"

"A ticket, a train ticket to go to the coast. Imagine, Dan, I'll see Vancouver and the Pacific Ocean!" In the excitement of Dan's gift, Scott had almost forgotten about his other wonderful present.

"Luck-eee," Dan exclaimed. Then he sighed. "Some day I'll go too."

"Yes, some day we'll go together. And not only to Vancouver, but to the north and all the way east to the Atlantic Ocean. As soon as we finish school, we'll get jobs and we'll travel together. We'll see the whole of Canada, and then..." Scott stopped, for what he wanted to say was "Then the map inside me will be all lit up, every last bit of it," but this was something he couldn't talk about, not even to his best friend, this feeling he had about Canada.

"Then what?" Daniel prompted.

Scott shrugged. "Then we'll know about everything in Canada from coast to coast, I guess. Come on, Dan, I'll show you my ticket, and I can't wait to show this mask to Jake."

Chapter 3

A Strange Warning

How slowly the days passed! Scott and Jake were to leave the very day after school closed, and Scott found it almost impossible to keep his mind on math and science and the capitals of Europe. The last few days were the worst of all. The school clock dragged its hands through the hours as though it had no wish to face the lonely months of vacation. But at last it was really and truly the last day. When Scott came home from school there were new clothes on the bed.

"Well, you couldn't go to Vancouver in those old jeans," Jake said. "I have my pride!"

Via Rail was coming through Lytton at 01.55. "You'll have to go to bed early this evening and try to get a little sleep," Jake said. "I'll wake you when it's time to go."

"What if you sleep through?"

"I won't. Oh, and Granny McKay says that Dan can come to see us off."

"Great. But I don't think I'll be able to go to sleep."

After supper Scott went to Daniel's house to say good-bye to Granny McKay. "Jake says you can come to see us off," Scott said to Dan.

"I know," Dan said. He didn't sound too happy.

Scott looked at him. "Hey, don't feel bad. I'm only going for two weeks and then I'll have all kinds of stuff to tell you."

"I suppose," Dan said, and added, "but I *am* glad for you, Scott. Come on in, there's cocoa and Gran's made your favorite almond cookies for you."

At the kitchen table, Scott and Dan sampled the cookies and drank their cocoa. Granny McKay sat opposite the boys, and her eyes, resting on Scott, had a strange look.

"Why are you looking at me like that, Granny?" Scott asked.

"Like what?" she replied, picking up her mug of coffee and sipping it slowly.

"Kind of funny," Scott said.

Mrs. McKay looked uncomfortable. "I can't tell you because you'll laugh at me," she said. "Dan does."

"No, I won't. Really I won't," Scott cried. "Please tell me."

"It's just that — well, Scott, even though I speak English and have a European name, I'm still Indian, and I'm not a young person with new ideas. There are some things that worry me, things that you or Jake would never think about or understand."

"Like what? What kinds of things?" Scott pressed.

Dan sat chewing a cookie and looking embarrassed.

For a while his grandmother quietly sipped her coffee, without answering Scott. At last she said, "You've always loved the river, haven't you, Scott?"

"Of course."

"You belong among us."

"Sure I do."

"And now you're going to the sea."

"Right."

"Well...just be careful," Mrs. McKay said.

"Gran believes in spirits," Dan burst out.

"What's that got to do with me going to the sea?" Scott asked, mystified.

"She thinks the ocean spirits might put some kind of spell on you because you like the river best, because you belong here." Dan turned to his grandmother. "Gee, Gran, nobody believes that stuff any more."

"Lots of people believe in spirits," Granny McKay said quietly. "Not only Indian people."

"Well, *people*-spirits maybe," Dan said, "but *water*-spirits?"

His grandmother looked at him for a few moments, and then a little past him in that thoughtful way she had. "These beliefs are not as simple-minded as you imagine," she said. "When you assign a spirit to something, it's a symbol of respect. Your ancestors believed that if you disregard the natural order of things, or are untrue to your own nature, you pay for it." Then she suddenly laughed. "But perhaps Dan's right," she said to Scott, "I shouldn't think about those things."

But Scott wasn't laughing. He respected Granny McKay too much to take her beliefs and forebodings lightly. Scott had always been fascinated by the legends and tales of the Native people. And he knew that even though Dan tried to sound scornful, he wasn't nearly as indifferent as he pretended to be; Dan had been excited enough about the legendary magic of the masks. Both he and Dan had heard many stories around camp fires and fireplaces that had given Scott the kinds of feelings he was sure Granny McKay was trying to express.

"How should I be careful, Gran?" he asked. "What do you mean?"

23

"I don't even know exactly," she replied. "Watch everything, Scott. Remember to use your head."

"All right, Granny," Scott said, "I'll remember."

"I wish you'd stop talking like this," Dan said. He was upset. His face had darkened, and there was a hint of tears in his eyes.

"All right, Dan, we won't say any more about it," Granny said. "It's just that if I feel anxious about Scott I have to tell him. Scott is like another grandchild to me." She didn't say any more.

But her words sank into Scott's mind, and that evening, when he lay in bed trying to sleep, he kept thinking about them. Granny McKay did seem to know some things in a way that no one else did. She read the weather better than the weather forecasters, and sometimes she could see events in people's past just by looking at the person. Quite often she could tell what you were thinking. Granny said that some people just knew things like that, felt them in their bones; she couldn't explain it. But for Pete's sake, what could possibly happen to him on his trip? He would be with Jake. No one would dare to harm Jake O'Burn's boy. Probably it was all nonsense, just as Dan had said. So Scott pushed the uneasiness that Granny McKay had awakened in him well to the back of his mind—and fell asleep.

In what seemed no time at all, Scott wakened to the sound of Jeremiah's old jeep, with Dan in the back, coming to take them to the station. Soon Jake and Scott and Jeremiah and Dan were rattling their way through the dark forest. When they emerged from among the trees, the stars hung low and huge over the river. No one said very much.

The railway station was chilly. Jake went to speak to the man at the wicket—trains stopped at Lytton only on

24

request — and Scott and Daniel sat down on the edge of the station bench beside the suitcases. Scott looked around at the few people who were also waiting for the train to Vancouver.

He wondered how these people could possibly appear so unexcited at the prospect of a journey to the coast. There was a young woman with a baby, who yawned continually. There was a man in a smart blue suit who read a newspaper with a great scowl across his forehead.

"Maybe I don't look excited either," Scott thought. "Maybe these people are all bubbling inside but not showing it on their faces." He hitched himself up in his seat to look at his own reflection in the glass of the station door. He saw a thin face with brown eyes staring back at him. "I guess I *don't* look very excited," he thought, "and I forgot to brush my hair," for the reflection also showed a great reddish tangle on the top of his head.

The station clock was just as slow-moving as the school clock had been. Surely it had been a quarter to two for ever and ever. Would the hands never move? Daniel, too, glanced at the clock once in a while, but he didn't say anything. Then, suddenly, they heard it, the faraway whistle, which was familiar enough at home in bed but which now sounded entirely different because it had something special to say to each of them.

"Come on, Jake," Scott cried, jumping up, "it's coming!"

Jake was talking to the station attendant. "Don't worry," he said, laughing at Scott, "we won't miss it."

"I'll help you with your stuff," Daniel said, hiding his eyes from Scott.

In a few moments, rattling and hissing, the train was at the platform, and Scott was boarding it, really and

25

truly boarding it, just like the people he saw in magazines who travelled on trains.

"Bye, Dan," he cried, stumbling over his suitcase. "Bye, Jeremiah. Come on, Jake," he urged, for Jake was taking his time.

In the car, Jake lifted their suitcases up onto the rack, and they both peered out of the window to wave. Then with a great jerk and rumble, the train began to move once more along the tracks. Scott was on his way to the Pacific Ocean.

They had comfortable reclining seats, but Scott did not intend to sleep. The dark rushed past him. The train sped past Boston Bar and Hell's Gate, thundering through tunnels and over trestles. Once in a while it stopped with a great lurch, disgorged some passengers, took on new ones, and then with a mighty heave started up again. Scott wanted to see the dawn, but in spite of himself he dozed off. When he woke up, they were stopped at Hope, and it was bright daylight. Soon they were off again.

"I'm starving," Scott said to Jake. "Aren't you hungry?"

"Sure am," said Jake. "Just waiting for you to wake up."

Staggering and swaying they made their way to the diner. Scott felt very important ordering bacon and eggs and pancakes and coffee from a real menu. While he ate, he kept his eyes on the view of the Fraser Valley opening in great sweeps of fields and pastures. Soon after breakfast, they entered the outskirts of Vancouver, and, at last, with a slackening of speed, they reached the railway yards, with their network of tracks, and the clatter and bustle of the big-city terminal.

With a shudder and a lurch the train came to a stop.

"There's Sandy," Scott yelled. Forgetting his suitcase, he raced down the steps to greet a tall man with a big head of shaggy, white hair.

Sandy gave him a warm hug. "Good to see you, kid," he said.

"Hey," Jake yelled from the train, "how about your suitcase?"

Laughing and talking, they drove through the busy streets of Vancouver, then sped over the Lions Gate Bridge with the inlet shimmering in the sun on either side of them. Scott looked down at the boats, made tiny by the height of the suspension bridge. Beyond the bridge, large ships from all over the world lay anchored, waiting for their turn at the loading docks. Scott felt as if he were on top of the world. In the bright sunlight Granny McKay's warnings seemed very far away.

Chapter 4

The Visitors

"Agnes Taylor next door has her sister and brother-in-law visiting her," said Mrs. Black to Jake and Scott as she prepared lunch. "Their name is Blair, they're from Seattle, and they're just rolling in money. They've been travelling all over the place."

Sandy and his wife seemed to know everything that was going on, and Jake was already up to date on all the latest news on the coast.

"These Blairs," Mrs. Black continued, "James and Amelia—you'll meet them—they're very nice. You'd never believe they were millionaires."

"Are they *millionaires*?" asked Scott, his eyes popping. "Real millionaires? You mean they've got a million dollars, actually?"

"More than a million, most probably," Mrs. Black said, nodding her dark head. "If you ask me, they probably have several."

Scott stared at her. Someone who was on speaking terms with millionaires was certainly a seven day's wonder, well worth a good stare.

"How come they're staying next door then?" he asked.

"Well, as I said, Agnes Taylor is Amelia Blair's sister," Mrs. Black repeated. "The Blairs are just here to visit Mrs. Taylor and her husband."

Scott wondered what it would be like to be a millionaire. You could have whatever you wanted. If he were one, he would buy a boat and a whole carton of oil paints. If you were a millionaire, you never thought about how much anything cost. You never had holes in your sheet in which your toe got stuck, and you went around everywhere in a Lincoln Continental. A millionaire never ate pork-and-beans (which was a pity in a way) or hot dogs. They ate asparagus and something called "pheasant-under-glass."

Scott pictured Mrs. Blair in his mind: she would be tall with golden hair braided around her head, and she would be dressed in blue velvet with a single strand of pearls around her neck, just like a commercial for fine wines or swanky cars. She would move slowly and have a longish kind of nose.

So when there was a quick, brisk knock on the door just after lunch and a lady of middle height with a short nose and very ordinary brown hair, dressed in jeans and a shirt, entered the kitchen in response to Sandy's hollered, "Come in," Scott simply could not believe that this was really the fabulous Mrs. Blair.

"Come in, Amelia," said Mrs. Black. "Meet our friends from up the Fraser Canyon. This is Jake O'Burn and Scott Anderson."

Jake shook hands with Amelia Blair, and then it was Scott's turn. He swallowed hard and took Mrs. Blair's hand. It was a firm hand, and the smile that accompanied it was open and direct.

"I'm glad to meet you," Mrs. Blair said. "So you're visiting Vancouver too. Is this your first visit?"

29

"Yes . . ." Scott's voice got caught somewhere in his throat. "Yes, it is," he repeated blushing.

"That's wonderful," said Mrs. Blair. She paid no attention to his embarrassment. "We'll all have lots of fun together. Whereabouts are you on the Fraser Canyon, Mr. O'Burn?"

"Jake's the name," Jake rumbled, and, glancing at him, Scott realized that Jake, too, was somewhat awed by the thought that he had just shaken a hand which could probably sign a cheque for ten thousand dollars or so with no hesitation whatever. "We're up by Lytton, Mrs. Blair, where the Thompson meets the Fraser. I run a little motel, Twin Rivers — nothing much to speak of, except that there's good fishing and interesting hiking trails around there."

Jake's words made Scott feel indignant. He did not like the way Jake belittled their motel.

"It's a lovely motel, Mrs. Blair," he said, finding his voice. "It overlooks the river, and you can climb down the rocks and fish in the pools, and the forest smells just wonderful."

"I'm sure it does," Mrs. Blair said, "and I'd just love to visit it."

"That would be great," Scott said. "We've got two empty cottages."

"But they're not good enough for you, Mrs. Blair," Jake said hurriedly. He looked a little worried. "There are many better motels than ours on the Trans-Canada. It's hot in the Canyon, 'specially round about Lytton."

"Hey, what kind of a business man are you?" Sandy shouted.

"I'm a truthful one," Jake laughed, but Scott could see that he was still worried.

Later Jake admonished Scott. "You hold your

tongue, Scotty," he said to him. "Those folks are not like us. They're used to the best."

Scott did not agree with him. "They don't have to stay if they don't like it," he said. "Besides they probably wouldn't even think of coming."

In the afternoon Scott went out to explore. The Blacks' home was pleasant, and, to Scott, used as he was to Jake's tiny cottage, it seemed huge. The house was set on a hillside in West Vancouver, overlooking the inlet. Above was a stretch of forest, too steep for homes. Always curious, Scott scrambled up the slope. A little farther on he found a clearing. He was on top of a small bluff. He looked around. It seemed to him that he was able to see at least halfway round the world.

Across the inlet, lay the city of Vancouver, serene and dignified, the many high-rises reflecting the afternoon sun. To his left, the two handsome bridges spanned the inlet. It must be great to be an architect or an engineer and create buildings and bridges, Scott thought.

To Scott's right, mists partly shrouded Point Atkinson and the waters beyond. Sandy had told him earlier that beyond that point lay the Strait of Georgia and Vancouver Island, on the other side of which was the great Pacific Ocean itself. They would go to see it for sure, Sandy had promised.

Briefly Granny McKay's warning flitted through Scott's mind, but he had no time to think about it, for he suddenly realized that he was not alone on the bluff. There had been a sound behind one of the bushes — a sneeze. Scott tiptoed round the bush. There, seated on a camp-stool before an easel, was a man, painting. Scott did not want to disturb him, but he was so interested that he crept forward step by step, trying to get a glimpse of

31

the painting. Try as he would to be silent, the man sensed his presence and glanced around.

"Hello," the painter said. He wore glasses, and the eyes behind the glasses remained serious, even though he smiled at Scott.

"Hello," Scott said, rather sheepishly. Then after a moment he added, "I'm sorry I disturbed you."

"That's all right," said the painter. "I'm nearly through anyway. I'm tired. I've been at this for hours."

Scott looked at the painting in awe. "That's great," he said.

The painter looked at his work, pursing his lips. "I don't really think so," he said. "No, it's not very good, I'm afraid. But I try — and try — and try. That's the most any of us can do. Right?"

The man took off his glasses, polished the lenses, and put them back on. Scott had not answered him. His eyes were fixed enviously on the oil paints.

"Do you live around here?" asked the painter, starting to clean his brushes.

"No," Scott said. "I'm here on a visit. I live up the Fraser Canyon."

"I visited the Canyon many years ago," said the painter, "at a time when I couldn't afford to paint. I have always promised myself that I would go back. Now I can afford to paint, but I'm afraid I've wasted too many years. I've lost the touch, somehow. It's very sad."

"Why didn't you paint then — long ago, I mean?"

"Because I had to make my living. I was travelling through to Alberta for an oil company. I had no time to stop. I had no time for anything in those days except making money."

"And did you make it?"

"Yes, I did. Lots and lots of it. But I lost my ability to paint."

Scott looked at the man without saying anything.

"I guess you're wondering why I want to paint pictures when I can afford to buy them. And much better ones too. Right?"

The painter always seemed to say "right" with a sort of snap.

"No," said Scott thoughtfully. He hesitated, then continued, "You see, I paint a bit too, and I make things out of wood, and I like my paintings and the things I make much better than anything I could buy—even though mine aren't as good."

The man scrutinized Scott through partly closed eyes.

"How old are you?" he asked.

"Twelve," Scott replied.

"Have some chocolate," the man offered.

He searched in his pocket and produced a candy bar, which he broke in two. He gave half to Scott.

"Come and sit down and tell me about your life in the Fraser Canyon," he said.

So Scott told the painter his name and about Jake and Twin Rivers, how he went to school with Dan, about his birthday and the train tickets and the mask that made him Dan's brother; about Flappy, and never having much money because of Jake's invalid sister in Regina and because there were always empty cabins in the motel. He had never talked so much to a stranger in his life, but this man seemed so interested. His serious eyes never once left Scott's face.

"So you're staying with Sandy Black," the man mused, when Scott ran out of things to tell. "What a coincidence."

"Do you know Sandy?" asked Scott, eagerly.

"I'm here on a visit too," said the painter. "We're staying with relatives. Right next door to you. My name is James Blair." He held out his hand. "How do you do, Scott Anderson?"

The man's hand was firm and friendly, just as his wife's had been.

Chapter 5

West to the Ocean

"Just think," said Scott to Jake that night, "I talked my head off and sat there eating chocolate and didn't even know he was a millionaire. Oh, I can't wait to tell Dan about it. I'll write him first thing tomorrow."

"Don't take Mrs. Black too seriously, Scott," laughed Jake. "I don't know if the Blairs are actually millionaires. They have a great deal of money to be sure, but Katy Black has a vivid imagination. The Blairs are very nice folk. That's what's important, not how much money they have."

"Oh, but I *like* to think they're millionaires," Scott cried. "It's exciting. It doesn't make them any less nice, just more interesting."

"Well, think what you like," Jake yawned, "but get to bed, for heaven's sake."

When Scott got up the next morning, he found that the Blairs had been invited to the Blacks' for breakfast. The Blacks' kitchen was flooded with sunlight, and Sandy Black was busy making hot cakes — his own recipe, the best in the Pacific Northwest, he assured them all. Katy Black was frying bacon, and scrambling eggs.

There was butter and jam on the table, as well as three kinds of syrup.

Mr. Blair smacked his lips as he sampled a hot cake heavy with butter and syrup. "The best in the west indeed," he said. He looked more cheerful this morning than he had up on the bluff the day before, when his painting had not been going too well.

Over breakfast, Scott learned that the Blairs had already been in Vancouver for several weeks, holidaying with their relatives. Now the Taylors were both back at work, and the Blairs were on their own during the day. The adults were busy making plans for Jake and Scott.

"I've still got two weeks of vacation left," Sandy said, "and I plan to take these two to Vancouver Island." He slapped a large hot cake down on Scott's plate. "And then across to Long Beach so that Scott can really see the ocean. We could camp there overnight. We'll go in my station wagon, and if you'd like to come," he added to the Blairs, "there'd be lots of room for you."

"Thank you," Mrs. Blair said, "I'd like to visit the Island again. But I don't think we'd go all the way to the ocean. What about that lovely lake near Port Alberni? You thought you'd like to make some sketches, James. We could stay in one of those little cottages."

"Sproat Lake," Mr. Blair supplied the name. "Yes, a charming spot. You could drop us there and when you come back from seeing the ocean, perhaps Scott would like to do some water skiing."

Scott's face lit up. "Oh, would I ever!" he cried.

Jake demurred a little. "That would mean renting a boat, wouldn't it?"

"You don't have to worry about that," Mr. Blair said quickly, "I'll be renting one anyway. I'd like to do some fishing."

36

"Well, if that's so . . . ," Jake said uncertainly.

"Absolutely," Mr. Blair declared.

"So that's all settled," Mrs. Blair smiled. "We'll start out early tomorrow, shall we?"

Scott couldn't wait for tomorrow to come. He had never been on a ferry large enough to carry three hundred and fifty cars. He wrote to Dan: "I'm seeing so many new things my head's all in a muddle. Tomorrow we're going across the Strait of Georgia to Vancouver Island and then on to the ocean. Wish you were here." He described all the people he had met in detail. "You should see Sandy Black's fancy house. They've got a dishwasher and everything, and three bathrooms. Imagine, three, and when you flush the toilets they don't make any noise. I know, I've tried them all."

In the afternoon Sandy Black took Jake and Scott on a tour of Vancouver. After lunch they met the Blairs at the Anthropology Museum at the University of British Columbia. Mr. Blair had been there once before but he wanted to make a more detailed study of the totem poles and he was sure that Scott would enjoy the museum.

The museum was on the outskirts of the campus and it commanded a magnificent view of water and mountains. But it was the contents of the museum that made Scott's mouth open in amazement.

He had never seen a real totem pole. Once Jake had bought him a small replica in a gift store, but he had never realized how impressive a real totem pole could be, how strong, how full of a special closeness between nature and the Native people of the coast. Scott could not put these feelings into words, but he could scarcely pull himself away from the totem poles. It was as though some magic had sprung to life and was holding him spellbound.

Mr. Blair seemed pleased with Scott's reaction. He rested a hand on Scott's shoulder. "They're quite something, aren't they?" He turned to his wife. "Scott tells me that he's a painter and a wood carver too."

Mrs. Blair's brown eyes widened with interest. "If you want to paint or carve, or do anything like that," she said to Scott, "just don't wait as long as James did. Get started while you're still young."

"I'd like to," Scott said, "but painting materials are expensive. There's always wood around though, so I do a lot of whittling. There's not much to do in the winter after dark."

"Do you have a television?" asked Mrs. Blair.

"Yes, but just two channels."

"So maybe you read a lot."

"Quite a bit. And Dan and I play games," explained Scott.

"Who is Dan?"

"My best friend. He lives with his grandmother near us."

"What kind of games do you play?"

"In the winter? Chinese checkers, scrabble."

"Chess?" asked Mr. Blair.

"I don't know how to play chess," Scott said.

"Well, we'll have to remedy that," Mr. Blair said. "Maybe we'll have time for some lessons before you go home."

"I'd like that," Scott said.

"Right," said Mr. Blair.

They continued their tour of the museum, and Scott exclaimed at all the masks on display. He told Mrs. Blair about the mask Dan had given him and described it. "It's very special," he said, but he didn't say anything about the magic.

"Living was easier for the people on the coast," Mr. Blair said. "That's why they had more time for art than the people of the interior." As they strolled along, he told Scott about the coastal Indians.

What a lot Mr. Blair knew, Scott thought. He would store all the information away to discuss with Dan. Scott left the museum with regret, looking back over his shoulder at the magnificent totem poles at the entrance.

The next day the six of them were up early, packing and stacking suitcases, and camping gear for Jake, Scott, and the Blacks, into the station wagon.

"I'm not crazy about camping," Mrs. Black admitted, "but Sandy simply loves it. He's like a kid when it comes to sleeping out-of-doors."

"We'll rent a cottage big enough for you to stay with us," Mrs. Blair said. "Then we can all have a choice as to where we want to sleep when you come to the lake. Who knows, maybe I'll take a turn in the tent too."

"That's a great idea," Mrs. Black said, "but I know where *I'm* going to sleep!"

They drove out to Horseshoe Bay where the ferry to Nanaimo docked. Scott couldn't wait to get his first view of a real ferry. He had seen them in pictures and on television, but the real thing was a different matter. All the cars were lined up in long rows, waiting for the ferry to arrive. People sat in their cars, reading newspapers or chatting, and some lounged around outside leaning on their cars, eating ice cream, or drinking pop or coffee. They all seemed so disinterested, just like the people at the train station had been, not at all impressed by the fact that they were about to board a ferry that could carry three hundred and fifty cars!

When Scott heard the deep blasts from the approaching vessel, he scrambled up on to the hood of

39

Sandy's station wagon to get a good view of it. How grand the ferry looked, moving slowly into the dock. It was called the Queen of Cowichan and did indeed look like a queen.

After the ferry had pulled away from the dock, they stood at the front with the wind trying to tear their hair out of their scalps and their jackets off their backs.

"It may be summer," Mrs. Blair said, "but this wind's too cold for me. I'm going in."

"I think I've had enough, too," said Mrs. Black. "I'll join you."

Mr. Blair was enjoying himself. He pointed out different types of boats to Scott. He had to shout to make himself heard against the wind. "That's a fishing trawler," he told Scott, "and that boat has crab traps out, you can tell by that row of bobbing things, and over there, far to your right, you can see a tug coming. It'll have a barge behind it."

"Do you live close to the sea, Mr. Blair?" Scott asked.

"We live in Bellevue, on Lake W——. It's on the other side of the lake from Sea—— ——ave a boat and we often go out to the sea. A—— ——rvous in the boat—she can't swim, you se—— ——e water much—but she wears a life jacket, —— ——he sea. You'll have to come and visit us som——

Scott, too, loved the wild sea w—— ——him, the spray flying, the sea gulls screami—— ——im, the sunlight scattering diamonds and —— ——ws on the blue water. He thought he could —— ——y forever.

But soon everyone got a bit hungry —— all trooped down to the cafeteria for hamb——rgers and French fries. Scott remembered the ideas he had had

40

about millionaires eating only things like pheasant and asparagus, but Mr. Blair was certainly enjoying that hamburger just as much as he had enjoyed Sandy's hot cakes.

Long before Scott was ready for it, the ferry had arrived at Departure Bay in Nanaimo, and it was time to disembark. Once off the ferry, Sandy drove to Sproat Lake. On the way they passed Nanoose Bay and Parkesville and Little Qualicum Falls, all magic names to Scott, all lighting up like little panel indicators on his secret map. At Sproat Lake they dropped off the Blairs.

"I'll be looking forward to that bed in the cabin when I get back," Mrs. Black laughed.

Then Sandy, Katy, Jake and Scott continued on their way to the west coast, to Long Beach.

At last Scott was going to see the real ocean.

Chapter 6

A Big Surprise

As they drove on to the coast, Scott felt sorry that the Blairs had not come with them. They had been fun, and it was the first time that strangers had taken so much interest in him. It made him feel important. He was about to say so when Jake, who was in the back seat with him, put an arm around his shoulders and gave him a little squeeze. "Having a good time, fellah?" he asked. And suddenly Scott realized that he had been paying very little attention in the last couple of days to the person he loved most in the world—Jake, who had made the whole fabulous holiday possible.

He grinned at him. "A marvellous time. Thanks, Jake."

"Nice people, those Blairs," Jake said. There was a funny little catch in his voice.

"They're okay," Scott said guardedly.

"Look at that hillside," Sandy Black interrupted from the driver's seat. "There's been a fire there some time ago."

Scott looked out of the window to see a whole hillside covered with ghostly, grey trunks of trees that must have met their end in a horrifying blaze.

"The bush is starting to come alive again, though," Mrs. Black said. "Look at all the greenery pushing up around the dead trees."

The adults chatted about this and that, but Scott, who had already begun to feel sleepy on the drive from the ferry to Sproat Lake, dozed off. And then, all of a sudden, Jake was shaking him. He opened his eyes, and there it was. The Pacific Ocean.

It was a brilliant day, and as far as eye could see, the ocean stretched, a shimmering blue-green, with dazzling white breakers racing in to crash against the endless stretch of silvery sand. Sea gulls soared and plummeted and screamed with the harsh voices that were already familiar to Scott.

"Oh, Jake," Scott said in a small voice, slipping his hand inside Jake's, something he hadn't done for a long time. He was glad to be seeing the ocean for the first time with Jake.

They found a place to park the station wagon and pitch their tent. Leaving the grown-ups to deal with those matters, Scott raced across the sand to the edge of the water. He plunged his arms into the eager, incoming waves and was surprised at their power. He nearly toppled over backwards. And cold! He hadn't thought the ocean would be so cold.

Katy Black, who had followed him, huddled in her jacket. "It's always cold here," she said, "even in midsummer. *I'm* going to sleep in the station wagon."

"All the more room for us in the tent," Sandy laughed.

He had brought a frisbee, and they had lots of fun racing after it as the wind blew it every which way over the sand. When the grown-ups tired, Scott walked along the beach looking for sea shells for Dan and found many

fascinating ones. Then they collected driftwood and made a fire.

"We'll have to turn in pretty early," Jake said. "It usually gets foggy around here after sunset. You can already see the mists forming out there."

Scott looked across the water, and sure enough it was no longer as brilliant as it had been earlier. Mist hung on the horizon, and the sun had become a little dimmer.

"Well, let's make supper. I guess we're all pretty hungry," Katy Black said.

And they were. Starving. Never had pork and beans and hot dogs tasted so good, or the coffee Katy made in an old pot, or the gingersnaps and peanut butter cookies she had baked herself.

By the time they had finished eating, the whole ocean had changed its character. It had become gloomy and filled with foreboding. The mists were rolling in fast. The sun had disappeared.

Scott and the two men crawled into the tent and Katy retired to the station wagon. Jake and Sandy chatted for some time in low voices and then fell silent.

Scott half dozed. The waves were pounding incessantly on the beach, and it seemed to him that he could hear strange, lonely cries, half muffled by the fog. He was suddenly reminded of Granny McKay's warnings and for the first time, they took on a frightening reality. Little spidery chills crawled up and down Scott's spine. He slept finally, but his sleep was full of troubled dreams.

But in the morning the sun was out again, and Scott's fears disappeared with the mists and his dreams. He helped to take down the tent and pile everything into the station wagon.

"Thanks, Sandy," Scott said. "Thanks for showing me the Pacific Ocean. I'll sure have a lot to write to Dan about."

They had breakfast at a small café and then drove back to Sproat Lake. By noon they were being greeted with enthusiasm by the Blairs.

"So was the ocean still there?" Mrs. Blair teased, ruffling Scott's hair.

"It was fantastic," Scott said. "We had a campfire and everything." But he said nothing about the rolling fog and the voices he had heard in the night. Even the memory of that was too disturbing. And he certainly did not want to talk about it.

"Did you do any painting?" he asked Mr. Blair.

"Just a few sketches. I'll show them to you later. But I managed to rent a boat so we can try that skiing. You'd like that, right?"

"Right!" Scott laughed, imitating Mr. Blair's clipped expression.

Scott changed into his trunks and ran out to the lake. Mr. Blair and Sandy were in a small motor boat in the water. Jake helped Scott with his ski belt and showed him how to put on the skis. They felt strange and clumsy. Scott half swam, half waded out to the boat.

"All right now," Mr. Blair said, throwing him the tow-line, "you hang on to that. We'll start up slowly at first, and you try to hold on. Your skis should be at an angle to the water. If they're too flat you'll fall on your face, and if they're too far out of the water you'll never get up. Ready?"

"Ready." Scott laughed with excitement and some nervousness.

Mr. Blair started up the motor and the boat moved out. As the rope grew taut, Scott tried to get his skis in

46

the position Mr. Blair had described. For a wonderful moment he thought he had succeeded at first try, but then Mr. Blair revved up the engine a little. Scott, pulled up suddenly and flopped flat on his face in the water, just as Mr. Blair had warned him, skis flapping all over the place. From the shore Jake laughed and called, "Try again, Scotty!"

"Okay. Again," Mr. Blair called over the noise of the motor.

Scott got his feet back into the skis, and once more the boat moved forward—and Scott promptly fell forward again with a great splash.

Over and over again he tried, until he felt he would never succeed, never reward Mr. Blair's patience. But then, all of a sudden, everything fell into place—his balance, the angle of the skis, his hold on the rope. He was skiing, yes, actually skiing across the blue surface of the lake. It was marvellous. It was like flying.

"Bravo," shouted Mr. Blair and Sandy from the boat, and "hurray and bravo" came from Jake and Katy and Mrs. Blair from the shore—and at that glorious moment Scott crashed again.

But he had done it. For those few wonderful moments he had actually skied on the water!

That evening, the Blairs invited them all to eat at the fancy dining room of a nearby hotel. They had to celebrate Scott's success, they said. Everyone got a bit dressed up, and Scott felt nervous. He had never been to a fancy dining room.

"Do I look okay?" he asked Jake.

"If they ask me what in heck you are, I'll tell them I dragged you out of the Pacific Ocean," Jake laughed. Whereupon Scott punched him, and they all went off laughing and in high spirits.

It was dark in the dining room, where little candles flickered on the tables and men with bow ties glided around carrying trays of wine and food. Scott had never seen such a menu and was at a loss for a few moments, but Mr. Blair came to his rescue quickly, explaining everything in a low voice so that Scott would not be embarrassed. He suggested that Scott have the cream of broccoli soup, the Cornish game hen and then choose his dessert when the time came. Scott was grateful to Mr. Blair for his tact and understanding, and he smiled to himself when he saw that the vegetable served with the game hen was asparagus.

Scott, Jake, and the Blacks spent the rest of their holiday at the lake, and by the end of that time Scott could ski with comfort and some skill. He went out every day and he couldn't get enough of it. Sometimes, early in the morning or in the evenings, Mr. Blair and Sandy, Jake, and Scott went fishing, and often caught something. They cooked the fish over the campfire, and with potatoes baked in the hot coals and with the special sauce Mrs. Blair made, it was delicious.

Some of the time Mr. Blair spent sketching. There wasn't enough time to start an oil, he said, and he encouraged Scott to make some sketches too. Scott was shy.

"You should have some pictures to take back for your friend," Mr. Blair said. This put Scott more at ease, and he made a few sketches of the lake and the boat and people on the shore. Mr. Blair watched his work with interest, giving him one or two hints for improving it. Mrs. Blair was delighted with Scott's pictures.

"Can I have one?" she asked. "I love this one with the little boy and the dog."

"Of course," Scott grinned. He flushed, proud that

Mrs. Blair had actually wanted one of his sketches. The Blairs certainly knew how to make a guy feel good.

Too soon it was time to go back to Vancouver. They were to go via the Malahat Highway and Victoria, the capital city of British Columbia. There were more sights to be seen in Victoria, and Jake took Scott to see the Legislative Building and the museum while the Blairs and the Blacks visited friends.

As they walked through the museum, Jake put an arm round Scott. "It's pretty good having you to myself again," he said.

Later, as they waited for the ferry to come in, Scott took out his sketch pad. He was no longer shy about his drawing. While the ferry docked, he made a quick sketch of it. "I found quite a good piece of wood by the lake," he said. "I want to make a model of the ferry for Dan. He'd like that."

"We haven't seen any of your wood work," Mrs. Blair said.

"I might get this finished before we leave," Scott said.

Mrs. Blair, who was sitting next to him in the car, gave him a little hug. "You've been a good companion, Scott," she said.

"Thanks," Scott said, feeling a bit embarrassed but very pleased.

On the last day of their stay, Mr. Blair took Scott to the art gallery in Vancouver. There was a special exhibition of the paintings of Emily Carr that Mr. Blair wanted to see. Mr. Blair told Scott that Emily Carr was the most famous of all west coast painters. Scott had never been to an art gallery.

The art gallery was quiet and rather dim. The paintings were individually lighted and hung like great

49

moments in the artist's life. Scott had never seen such paintings, and the work of Emily Carr made him feel half happy and half sad. Though Mr. Blair seemed to expect it, Scott couldn't put the feeling into words. He was silent and listened intently to Mr. Blair talk about the artist and her paintings.

Mr. Blair knew a great deal about Emily Carr and told Scott how much the great painter had loved her native coast and how hard she had tried to catch its magic in her work.

"She herself was never satisfied with what she had done," Mr. Blair said. "She was always trying to capture the sense of God in the forests and she never felt she had succeeded. I suppose all good painters think they should do better."

Though Scott couldn't say it, he wondered to himself if this visit to the art gallery wasn't the best thing of all the things he had experienced on this holiday. He wished Jake and Dan had been there to share it.

That evening the grown-ups had another surprise for Scott. Scott and Jake were going home the next day, but they were not going alone and they were not going back by train. They were going in the Blairs' car! The Blairs were going to continue their holiday at Twin Rivers!

Chapter 7

Back at Twin Rivers

At Twin Rivers, Daniel was lonely for Scott. Nothing that he did was as much fun without Scott and even at home things felt different. His grandmother's thoughts seemed to be somewhere else and she wasn't her usual patient, loving self.

"Granny," Daniel said thoughtfully one morning, "what's the matter with you? Aren't you feeling well? You've been sort of queer ever since Scott and Jake left. You never get mad about silly things, but today you quarrelled with Jeremiah over which dish Flappy should use and yesterday you were cross with the lady in Number 3. I thought she'd leave for sure."

Mrs. McKay put her arms around her grandson. "I know, Daniel," she said. "I *have* been on edge lately and I'm sorry. I suppose it's because I'm not happy about Scott. I can't explain it, but I'm just not happy."

"But Granny, we've had cards and letters from Scott. He's fine. He's having fun. Why should you worry?"

"That's what I wish I knew," Granny said slowly. "That's just what I don't know. Why do I have this worry

51

gnawing at me all the time? Well, I'll just try to put it out of my mind. You're missing Scott too, and I should be thinking about you, not about Scott or myself. Now I've got to get to work and I'll try to be extra nice to that lady in Number 3."

But work didn't solve the problem. If Granny McKay did not believe in the power of the spirits in the way her ancestors had done, she did not scoff at it either. She had come to the conclusion that the world was not as simple as the people who laughed at such beliefs thought it was. Sometimes very strange things did happen, things for which no one had any explanation. Nobody had as yet solved the riddle of life to Granny's satisfaction. So when she had these strange feelings of disquiet she could not dismiss them lightly.

It was true that Scott's letters and cards were full of fun and exciting adventures. He seemed to be having a perfect holiday. What, then, was the meaning of the dark shadow that Granny saw so clearly moving behind Scott whenever she closed her eyes and pictured the boy she loved so well?

She had seen this shadow behind Scott when he had told her about his trip to the coast. That was why she had spoken about the ocean spirits. She had not been able to explain the shadow in any other way. Perhaps the spirits did not exist, but it was the only way Granny could express this power she felt in herself — this power to sense that all was not right.

The days passed slowly, but at last it was nearly time for Jake and Scott to return. Only a couple of days were left.

Annie McKay was going to Jake's cottage to make sure it was clean and tidy. As she passed the door of the motel office, she heard the phone ringing and Jeremiah

answering it with that voice of his that sounded like a rusty old saw biting into hard wood. She stopped, and saw that Jeremiah was listening, a grin on his grizzled face. When he hung up, Granny asked, "Who was that? Visitors, I hope." Business had not been very good.

"It was Jake," Jeremiah said. "They're coming home and bringing friends. It's those Blairs Scotty keeps writing about. Jake wants you to get Number 4 ready—the biggest cabin."

"All right," Mrs. McKay said. "I'll start it as soon as I finish with Jake's place."

Dan was mowing the lawn just outside the motel office, a chore he had volunteered to do for Jeremiah.

"Scott and Jake are coming home," Granny told him brightly, "and they're bringing their friends, the Blairs."

"Scott sure seems hung up on those Blairs," Daniel said. He picked up a pebble uncovered by the lawn mower and threw it hard against a tree trunk.

"I suppose they've been good to him," his grandmother replied.

"I guess," Daniel said.

"Come and give me a hand with Number 4 when you're through with the grass," his grandmother said. "We'll make a better job of it together."

By the time Jake and Scott and their visitors were due to arrive, Number 4 was spotless. The floors had been scrubbed, the furniture dusted and polished, the beds freshly made up. Outside, Jeremiah had trimmed the postage-stamp lawn and cleared the flower beds of old blooms. He had swept the path and washed the table and the two chairs on the tiny veranda. Daniel had brought in an armful of forest flowers, which Granny McKay arranged in a big vase on the dresser.

It was nearly four in the afternoon when Daniel

heard the crunching of gravel under heavy car wheels. Scrambling onto his lookout rock, he saw a big grey car travelling slowly and carefully along the narrow road to the motel; it had to be Jake and Scott and their friends.

Daniel slid down the rock and started towards the car, which ground to a stop just outside Number 4. But then Daniel paused, suddenly overcome with shyness. The grey car looked so impressive, so much from another kind of world. What would Scott's fine new friends think of him? Maybe he would wait and see how things were, what these friends were like. He stayed hidden among the trees.

But as he was hesitating, Scott jumped out of the grey car and ran down the path shouting: "Dan, Dan, where are you? Dan, I'm home!"

And when Dan realized that Scott was actually racing in the direction of his house, he ran out of his hiding place and called to Scott, "Hey, I'm here."

Scott made an about turn and raced back to meet Dan halfway. They grasped hands and swung each other around.

"Did you see what I came in?" Scott cried. "Come and look!"

Daniel hesitated again, uncertainty in the pit of his stomach. He hung back.

"Come on," Scott urged him. "These are the Blairs I told you about in my letters. You'll like them. They've come to stay here. Mr. Blair's going to paint. I've got a million things to tell you. Come and meet them."

But Dan pulled his hand free of Scott's. "Not now, Scott," he said. "They won't want to be bothered. Please, not now."

"Oh, Dan," Scott cried, "what's come over you?" But seeing the look on Dan's face, he said, "Okay then;

55

let's go and see Gran. I'll introduce you to my friends later."

So the two boys raced off through the woods to Granny McKay's house. Granny had made Scott's favorite almond cookies, and tall glasses of lemonade were already poured for them. He gave Granny a big hug and then started talking. He just couldn't stop. There was so much to tell.

"What have *you* been doing, Dan?" he asked his friend at last. "Tell me all the news."

But Daniel had become strangely silent while his friend had been talking, and he couldn't think of anything much to tell Scott.

"Nothing's changed around here. I caught quite a few fish last week. Granny had a cold, and Jeremiah fell and hurt his ankle, but they're both better now. And the baby robins are all grown up."

"Let's go and see our cave," Scott said. "I missed it. I missed everything, even in the middle of all the fun I was having. I thought of you a lot. Honest. Let's go say hello to the river. Oh, Dan, you ought to see the ocean — glittering, right to the horizon. It's beautiful. But come on, let's go paddling."

The two boys ran through the woods and in front of the cottages with their little squares of grass and flowers, but before they could get away, a voice called to them from Number 4.

"Scott, my lad." It was Mr. Blair. "Would you come here a minute?"

Scott turned in his tracks and jogged back to cabin Number 4, Dan following him at a distance.

"Mrs. Blair will need an extra pillow, Scott. Do you think you could ask Jake or someone if we could have one?"

"Sure," Scott said, then added, "Mr. Blair, I'd like you to meet Dan. He's my best friend. Come here, Dan."

Daniel walked up to Scott. He could feel his heart beating from sudden anxiety.

"Hello," he said, breathlessly.

"Hello, Dan," Mr. Blair said with a smile, holding out his hand. Daniel put out his own hand, a little hesitantly, and Mr. Blair took it in a firm grasp. They looked at each other, Scott's tall American friend, and his slim, sun-tanned friend of the woods and the river, and for some reason a shiver ran down Scott's back in spite of the fact that he was hot from running.

Mrs. Blair came out of the cottage and stood beside her husband.

"Amelia, this is Dan, Scott's best friend," Mr. Blair said. "Dan, this is my wife."

"Hello," Dan said again. He wished his knees didn't feel as though he had to sit down.

"I'm glad to know you, Dan," Mrs. Blair said.

She, too, spoke in a friendly way, but for some reason Scott suddenly found himself wishing that Dan had worn a shirt and that his jeans weren't quite so ragged. There was a great smear across his forehead too.

"I'll get you an extra pillow, Mrs. Blair," Scott said. "Right away. Come on, Dan." And taking hold of Dan's arm, Scott started off to race him back to Gran's. She was the one who looked after pillows.

On the way, they passed Jake's cabin, and looking in for a moment, Scott saw that Jake had taken in the suitcases and was opening them.

"I got some things for you, Dan," Scott said. "I'll get them out of my suitcase. Look, why don't you ask Gran for that pillow and take it over to Mrs. Blair, and I'll get your stuff out."

"All right," Dan agreed, although his heart sank a little at the thought of the Blairs. "Where shall I meet you?"

"At the cave," Scott said, "and then we'll go down to the river."

Dan took a pillow out of Gran's store cupboard and trudged off to Number 4. It was a bulky pillow, and he hugged it to his bare, brown body. It felt cool against his stomach. Flappy saw him and ran after him, jumping and tugging at the pillow. "Get away," Dan said, "get away, Flap." He was nearly at the door when Mrs. Blair came out of the cabin.

Dan stood speechless before Mrs. Blair, still hugging the pillow.

"Is that my pillow?" she asked. Dan nodded. "Thank you," Mrs. Blair said, smiling. She took the pillow from Dan. There was a little silence.

Dan said, "I hope it's okay."

Mrs. Blair looked at the pillow. "I'm sure it is, Dan — why shouldn't it be?"

"Flappy — that's Scott's dog — jumped up on it," Dan said in a rush. "There's a bit of dirt on it . . ." Dan flushed.

Mrs. Blair rubbed the offending smudge. "Oh, I don't think that spot of dirt will bother me," she said.

She's pretty, Dan thought, and nice. Why do I feel so awful? Why don't I like her more? He shifted from one bare foot to the other, curling his toes.

"Well, we'll see you around, Dan," Mrs. Blair said. "Thank you very much for the pillow."

"You're welcome," Dan said. Then he ran off to meet Scott in their cave.

Chapter 8

Moods and Misgivings

It was some time before Scott joined him. Dan sat at the cave entrance, his bare toes scrabbling in the dust, the sunlight and leaf shadows speckling his body. He could feel the coolness of the cave behind him. He had so looked forward to Scott's homecoming, and now, somehow, the joy had gone out of it. Dan didn't know why he felt like that.

At last Scott appeared. He had made some sandwiches so that they could have a picnic in the cave. Scott had the sandwiches in one hand and in his other he carried a brown paper bag.

Scott put the sandwiches on a flat rock. Then he held out the paper bag to Daniel.

"For you," he said.

Dan's eyes lit up. "What is it?" he asked.

"Stuff," Scott said. "Come on, open it."

There was a fine pocket compass with a picture of a totem pole on the back and a postcard album with pictures of the coast from Vancouver to Alaska. There was the box of shells that Scott had collected on Long Beach. And there was the model of the ferry that Scott had carved for Dan.

"It's for your birthday too," Scott said. "We missed it. The compass and the album are from Jake, and I collected the shells on the very edge of the Pacific Ocean. Then I made the boat. It's a ferry and it goes between Vancouver and Vancouver Island. It takes three hundred and fifty cars."

"They're great — just great." Dan's eyes glowed. "You don't mind if I like the boat best, do you?"

"Do you really like it best, Dan?" Scott asked. "Mr. Blair thought it was sort of good too."

At the mention of Mr. Blair, Dan's face changed. The glow faded from his eyes. The sunlight streaming through the door of the cave seemed to dim a little.

"What's the matter?" Scott asked, sensing something was wrong.

"Nothing," Dan said. "Nothing at all. It's just that . . . that . . . you brought me so many things, I'm all excited, I guess." How could he explain to Scott the strange case of jitters he experienced every time Scott's new friends were mentioned? Scott would think he was crazy.

Later, after they had had their picnic lunch, and after they had been down to the river and Scott had once again felt its chill waters lap round his ankles, the boys made their way home. The Blairs were sitting out on the porch in front of their cabin enjoying the evening air. Jake was perched on the porch rail, talking to the Blairs.

"Home to bed?" asked Mr. Blair.

"Just about," Scott said. He tossed and caught a little pebble he had picked up by the river. Mrs. Blair held out her hand.

"Show me what you've got," she said. "Did you find something interesting?"

Scott came closer and stood by her chair.

"Just a pebble from the river," he said. "This one's a bit different, though. I'm going to break it in half and look it up in my rock book to see what it is."

Mrs. Blair looked at the rock and then returned it to Scott.

"Let me know when you find out," she said. Then she reached up and pulled Scott's face down towards her, kissing him lightly on the forehead.

"Good night," she said.

Daniel, hovering in the background close to the bush, swallowed hard. Then he turned and ran home through the trees, like a wild thing alarmed by something it didn't understand.

No one heard him go. Scott lingered with the Blairs and Jake. "Do I have to go to bed?" he asked.

"You have to," Jake said. "You'd think you'd be half dead by now, you've had such a long day. But James, Amelia . . . I was wondering if you'd come over to my place for a cup of coffee. I do pride myself on my coffee."

"We'd love to," Amelia Blair said.

"Get along, Scotty," Jake said, and by the tone of his voice Scott knew that he meant it this time.

"Good night everyone," he said, and ran off.

By the time the Blairs and Jake had strolled over to Jake's place, Scott was in bed, and even though he was determined to stay awake, sleep began to overcome him. Through a half-doze he heard the Blairs and Jake come into the cottage and all the sounds in the kitchen indicating that Jake was putting on the coffee pot and setting out coffee mugs on the kitchen table. He heard the voices of the grown-ups, but his thoughts, already mixed with dreams, were on the events of the day just past — the ride along the highway on the edge of the canyon, seeing Dan again, and Gran, and Flappy's unabashed joy at his homecoming.

And then suddenly Scott heard his name, carried from the kitchen into his bedroom in Mrs. Blair's clear voice. It broke through his near-sleep and jerked him wide awake.

What had Mrs. Blair said? Oh, why had he fallen asleep like that?

But Mrs. Blair was continuing, "I don't know if you fully realize just how unusually gifted your boy is."

Mrs. Blair was talking about him! *He* was Jake's boy! Unusually gifted! Mrs. Blair thought he was unusually gifted. *This* Scott had to hear, even though he knew it was wrong to eavesdrop. Except that he wasn't exactly eaves-dropping — Jake and the Blairs knew he was in the house and were making no effort to lower their voices.

"Sure, Scotty's a bright lad," Jake said in his slow way.

"No, we don't mean just bright," Mr. Blair said, picking up from his wife. "We mean talented. I saw that model he made of the ferry. And his sketches are excellent. He's only twelve. There's no telling how well he might do."

"The model *was* pretty good," Scott heard Jake growl — and Scott grinned. It was impossible for Jake to keep the pride out of his voice.

"Have you thought of giving him extra lessons?" Mr. Blair asked. "He should have every opportunity to develop his gifts. Believe me. You must speak to his teachers. Surely there's someone around here who could give him some instruction?"

"There probably is," Jake said, sounding a bit huffy. "But all these things cost a lot of money. Lots. Teachers and materials. And where will it lead? Scott must learn the kinds of things that will make him a living when he's grown. The frills will have to wait."

"That's not always the best way, Jake," Mr. Blair said quietly. "Sometimes we wait too long. I know."

There was silence in the kitchen for a few moments, broken only by the sounds of spoons clinking, of mugs touching on the coffee table, and of coffee burbling in the pot.

"Well, I'll give it some thought," Jake said finally. "Good of you to take an interest in old Scotty."

"Could I have some more of that coffee? It really is excellent, Jake." Mr. Blair's voice had regained its cheerfulness. "And those cookies are delicious."

"Made by Annie McKay — young Dan's grandmother. Marvellous cook."

"Your coffee *is* good, Jake," Mrs. Blair said. "No wonder Scott's got into the habit of drinking so much of it."

"Scotty? Do you think he drinks too much coffee?" Jake's voice sounded surprised and anxious.

"Maybe it's just a holiday treat," Mrs. Blair suggested.

There was a short silence in the kitchen.

"I suppose he has got into a few bad habits living with me," Jake said. "You're right. Coffee can't be good for him."

"It's not any of my business. I'm sorry," Mrs. Blair apologized quickly, and Scott could hear the smile in her voice. "It's just that I've become so fond of him."

The next morning Scott was up early, but Jake was already making breakfast.

"Now listen," Jake said, tapping his finger on the table to ensure Scott's attention. "Don't you go hanging around the Blairs. They're here for a holiday, and they don't want you under their feet every two minutes."

Scott promised, but he couldn't resist just walking past Number 4 to see what was happening. He didn't intend to stop. So when Mrs. Blair called him he didn't feel that he was disobeying Jake.

"Finished breakfast?" she asked.

Scott nodded. "Yep."

"Mr. Blair is fussing with his fishing gear," Mrs. Blair said. "I wondered if you'd show me around a bit."

"I'd love to, " Scott said. "We can go down to the river, and I'll show you our cave and we can go up to the stream where Dan and I catch fish."

"Good," Mrs. Blair said, "I'd like that. Just wait a few minutes till I get these dishes done."

"I'll help you," Scott said.

While they worked, they talked. Scott felt a little shy because of what he had overheard the night before. Jake always praised him for something well done, but it was different when the praise came from strangers. But Mrs. Blair did not mention the conversation.

"So Dan's your best friend," Mrs. Blair said. "Is he your only friend?"

"I'm friends with lots of boys and girls," Scott said, "but most of them live quite a-ways off. Dan's always here. And since he gave me that mask he's my brother."

Mrs. Blair nodded. "Where does he live?"

"Just a little way up the hill. Would you like to go and meet his gran?" he asked eagerly. "She's really like my gran too."

"Isn't it a bit early?" Mrs. Blair demurred.

"Gran's always up," Scott said.

"All right, I'd like to go," Mrs. Blair said.

They left the cabin and walked through the woods together.

"There it is," Scott said when they came in view of Dan's house. He ran to the door, knocking on it and flinging it open all in one motion.

"Gran! You've got a visitor," he called.

There was a clatter from the kitchen, then Annie McKay appeared.

"This is Mrs. McKay, Dan's Gran," Scott said. "Granny, this is Mrs. Blair."

"I'm pleased to meet you, Mrs. Blair," Gran said, taking Mrs. Blair's outstretched hand.

"I told Scott we were calling too early," Mrs. Blair said. "You must be busy."

"No, not at all," Granny McKay said. "Please sit down. Dan," she called, "we have visitors."

Daniel appeared and stood uncertainly by the door. "Hi," he said.

"Good morning, Dan," Mrs. Blair said. "I slept very well on the pillow you got for me." They both laughed, Dan uneasily.

Scott perched on the edge of the couch next to Mrs. Blair. "Gran does beautiful weaving," he said. "Would you like to see it?"

"I certainly would," Mrs. Blair said eagerly.

"Oh no, Scott," Granny McKay began, but Scott interrupted her. "Someone said that Gran's baskets and weaving and things are the best in the whole interior."

"Please show them to me, Mrs. McKay," Mrs. Blair begged.

So Granny McKay took Mrs. Blair into a back room and showed her her work. Some of it was ready for sale and some was still in progress.

"Scott's right, they're absolutely marvellous," Mrs. Blair declared. "May I buy some, please? They are for sale, aren't they? I'd love to take a few pieces home for my friends." And suddenly the two women were talking as though they had known each other all their lives.

Scott and Dan went outside.

"I think they're going to get on well," Scott said happily.

"I guess," Dan said. He picked up a stick from the ground and swung it forcefully at an overhanging tree branch.

Chapter 9

A Straight Flush and Laughter

The days passed quickly, as holidays always do.

Mr. Blair divided his time between fishing and painting. He took trips up and down the canyon to find good vantage spots and he often took Scott with him. He made good his promise and taught Scott the fundamentals of chess and was pleased with the quick way Scott caught on.

Mrs. Blair spent her time walking and reading. She did not swim and found the river too cold even for wading, although Scott showed her some pools where the sun warmed the water. She and Scott explored many trails together and found rocks and wild flowers and many curious plants that Scott had never noticed before Mrs. Blair pointed them out. Jake no longer told Scott not to "bother" the Blairs because they seemed to want Scott's company as much as he enjoyed being with them.

Scott didn't see Dan as much as usual because he knew the Blairs would be leaving soon and he wanted to spend as much time as he could with them.

"You can come too," he said to Dan again and again, but Dan would shake his head and say he had something else to do.

But now Scott was waiting for Friday. Friday was the night when Joe Fricton and Sammy Gore and Pete Boggle came up to Twin Rivers to play poker with Jake. Scott liked them and he hadn't seen them for a long time.

For this event, Scott and Jake made sandwiches on Friday morning. First there were peanut butter and jelly sandwiches. Scott would spread the peanut butter, Jake the jelly, and the two pieces would be slapped together with a squelch and packed back into the original bread-bag to keep moist. The second lot were bologna. Scott would spread the mayonnaise, Jake would hack off a slab of bologna, add tomatoes and lettuce and pickles, and then squeeze the sandwich down with his large hand so that the lettuce crackled and the mayonnaise squirted out at the sides. It was fun making the sandwiches, and Scott always looked forward to Friday and the arrival of Joe Fricton, Sammy Gore, and Pete Boggle. He was allowed to stay up as long as he liked to watch them play. Jake's friends had taught Scott a lot of things about cards, and then he taught Dan.

Friday came, and the men arrived at about eight o'clock in a creaky old Chevy.

When Scott had finished tidying up in the kitchen, he went out and talked to Mrs. Blair for a while. She was sitting outside her cabin, enjoying the pine-scented evening. Scott lay on the grass and told her all about Jake's three guests.

Joe Fricton had eight children and worked in a logging camp near Boston Bar. When he came home there were always so many people around and so many things to do that he never had a moment to himself. It was a real treat for Joe to get away for a night with Jake and the boys.

Sammy Gore had a grocery store in Lytton. His wife had arthritis and wasn't very cheerful. The neighbors said that she was always cranky with Sammy no matter how much he did for her. But Scott wasn't sure about that, and Jake told him that it wasn't right to gossip.

Pete Boggle had dentures, which he took out when they hurt him. They looked funny on the table all by themselves. Scott giggled.

Mrs. Blair was looking a little strange. "And what does Pete Boggle do?" she asked.

"Do? Oh, well, he doesn't *do* anything much. He doesn't have a family or even a wife. He gets odd jobs here and there. Sometimes the others call him a bum, but they're just teasing him. I really like Pete."

Scott looked up at Mrs. Blair from where he was lying on the grass and caught that strange look in her eyes. "I *really* like Pete," he repeated hastily. "He's *very* kind. Once when Flappy was awfully sick, Pete sat up with her all night. And when he has any money at all he shares it with all his friends."

Mrs. Blair nodded thoughtfully. "And these three — persons — are Jake's best friends?"

"I suppose so," Scott said. "Except Sandy, of course, and unless you count Jeremiah. But Jeremiah's too old. He thinks he's a hundred and two years old, but I don't think that's true, do you?"

"No, I don't think he's that old," said Mrs. Blair. "But Jeremiah certainly is very old, perhaps in his nineties. He shouldn't do any hard work. He's earned his right to sit in the sun. And he certainly shouldn't be driving that jeep."

"That's what Jake says, but Jeremiah says he'll work and drive his jeep till the day he drops dead."

Mrs. Blair nodded again, very thoughtfully. "Scott," she said, "these friends of Jake's, they're all good enough fellows, I'm sure, but they seem a little — well — rough. You should try not to talk like them. 'Bum' isn't a very nice expression. I'm sure your school teachers would say the same. You should model yourself on your teachers."

"I try to," Scott said, "most always, but these guys —Joe and Pete and Sam—they're all right too." He searched inside himself to try to find a way to explain what he meant to Mrs. Blair. "These guys," he repeated, then realized that this was another word that Mrs. Blair probably wouldn't like. "These friends of Jake's," he corrected himself, "I know they're not smart and fancy, but they're . . . they're like my favorite trees— sort of comfortable to be with." Scott couldn't say any more.

"I have to go now," he said after a while. "They start to play soon after they get here, and I like to watch them. They teach me all sorts of things about card-playing." Scott paused. Mrs. Blair's eyebrows had risen. She looked quite startled. "You wouldn't like to come and meet them, would you?" he asked.

"You'll have to excuse me," Mrs. Blair said, smiling in a tired way. "I've got quite a bad headache. I probably shouldn't have stayed in the sun so long. It's made me feel rather ill."

"Okay," Scott said, feeling disappointed. "D'you want anything?" he added, remembering his manners. "Can I get you something?"

"No. I'll be all right. I'll just have to get to bed early and have a good sleep. Thanks anyway, Scott."

As always, the men started their evening with jokes and teasing and back-slapping. Everyone wanted to hear about Jake's trip, but soon they settled down to the cards. There was silence while the game was in progress, but every so often there would be a shout when a good hand was shown.

Time passed quickly. Scott watched both TV and the game. At midnight, the movie he'd been watching off and on was over and he returned to the kitchen.

He was just in time to watch Pete Boggle make a straight flush, and there was a great burst of laughter and cheering, and everyone had another drink all round. Jake's kitchen was so thick with smoke that Scott's eyes watered dreadfully, but he wasn't going to go to bed. It was far too exciting. As usual he put on the coffee pot and got out the sandwiches.

Funny how Mrs. Blair had remarked on his drinking coffee, Scott thought. Maybe it *was* bad for him. Anyway, Jake had switched to cocoa in the evening and said that when Scott went back to school it would be cocoa in the morning too. Jake said that Mrs. Blair had suggested it, which Scott knew already, and he thought she was right. Jake thought a lot of Mrs. Blair. It wasn't because she was rich, Scott knew. It was because she was pleasant and had a lot of what Jake called "horse sense."

"Listen to this one I heard at Kippy's," Sam Gore chortled.

Scott never paid much attention to the jokes the men told, because he didn't understand most of them. This one must have been very funny, for they all roared. And at that moment there was a knock on the door.

"Come in," Jake hollered.

The door opened. Mrs. Blair stood on the step in her dressing gown. Jake rose from his chair.

"Jake," she said, apologetically, "I'm terribly sorry to disturb you, but I've got the worst headache and sounds do carry so clearly here at night. I hate to ask, but do you think you could be just a little bit more quiet? I simply can't fall asleep. It's just me, I know. It doesn't seem to be bothering James." She smiled, a little wryly. Then suddenly she saw Scott in the corner.

"Scott!" she exclaimed.

Scott stared at her. He saw the surprise on her face

and he was filled with dismay. But there was nothing he could say. He dropped his eyes. The coffee pot perked madly in the silence.

"I'm sorry," Mrs. Blair said with a little laugh, "but I didn't expect to see Scott up so late."

"He does stick around," Jake said heavily. He was embarrassed in front of his friends. "It's his special night," he added.

"Of course," Mrs. Blair said, "Scott told me, but I forgot. How silly of me."

"Amelia, these are my buddies," Jake said. "May I introduce you? Pete Boggle, Sam Gore, and Joe Fricton." In turn the men rose and greeted Mrs. Blair.

She came into the room then and shook hands with each in turn. "Hello," she said brightly. "Scott has told me all about you. I'm pleased to meet you. I just wish I was feeling better."

Everyone felt relieved. "I'm sorry, Amelia," Jake said. He twiddled the cards in his hands. "I'm real sorry. We'll try to keep it down. We'll be quiet enough for you to sleep. For sure."

"Thank you, " Mrs. Blair said. "That's kind of you."

After Mrs. Blair left, Scott passed round the coffee.

"Cocoa for you," Jake said, and something in his voice made Scott realize that cocoa it had to be, special night or not.

The next day, sitting at the entrance to their cave, Scott told Dan about the card night.

"I guess Jake's friends are sort of tough and noisy, but I like them a lot. Mrs. Blair was very polite to them, but I don't think she liked them much. I think a guy should know all kinds of people. So does Jake."

"Why should you care what Mrs. Blair thinks?" asked Dan.

Scott looked at Dan in surprise. "Because I like her, I guess. I like both the Blairs."

Dan made patterns in the sandy soil with the sharp point of a rock. "You know what I think?" he said.

"What?"

"Remember all that stuff Gran was telling us about spirits?"

"Sure."

"I think it's true."

"Dan! What do you mean?"

"You've changed, Scott, since you were away. You're not my friend any more. Not really. And it's those Blairs. They've changed you. Ever since you went to the coast. I don't like them. Maybe they're the ocean spirits Gran was talking about."

"Dan! You were the one who didn't believe Gran."

"I know. But I've changed my mind. Something weird's going on. Spirits can take different shapes. Who knows? Anyway, you're not the same person, Scott."

"I think you're plain nuts, Dan. Mr. Blair's not any spirit. He's a well-known business man."

Dan shrugged. "Well known or not, maybe the spirits sent the Blairs." Dan looked at Scott, and his eyes were bright with the tears he was holding back. Then he threw away the rock with which he had been making patterns in the sand and ran from the cave.

Scott was shaken. It had never occurred to him that Dan was feeling this way. He had always invited Dan to come whenever he went anywhere with the Blairs — well, almost always. But Dan had refused every time. Dan was jealous of his friendship with the Blairs.

Scott didn't know what to do. For the next few days he went out of his way to find Dan but Dan never seemed to be around. Granny McKay said that he was spending a lot of time with someone who lived on the other side of Lytton and she didn't see much of him either. Scott knew that Dan was avoiding him.

Scott was miserable. He liked the Blairs, of course he did, but he certainly would never trade Dan's friendship for theirs. There was no one in the world he liked as much as Dan, except Jake, but that was different. Dan should know that. Dan was part of him, more than a real brother.

A few evenings later, Scott made a decision. He would go to Dan's place.

Outside the motel, the pines looked black against the still-light sky. The firs, spiralling skywards, reminded Scott of Emily Carr's pictures. Somewhere a train rumbled, its lonely warning echoing through the dusk.

As Scott walked past cabin Number 4, he heard the Blairs and Jake talking. Their voices were pitched low, and they sounded very serious. Scott thought of the night when Mrs. Blair had been so shocked at seeing him at the card game. What were they talking about now, he wondered?

At Dan's house he knocked and went in.

Dan looked up, surprised. He was watching a TV show.

Scott said, "I've just come to tell you that if you don't like me being friends with the Blairs I won't see them any more than I have to. I'll only do things with you. I'll go with them only if it's rude not to. But otherwise I'll be with you. You're my best friend, Dan; more than that — you're my brother. You should know that. And I'm sorry if I hurt your feelings, but I didn't mean to."

Dan grinned a huge grin. Then he turned back to the TV. "Want to watch the end of this movie?" he asked.

Chapter 10

An Astonishing Proposal

When Scott left Dan's house, his heart felt lighter than it had for days. At home he got ready for bed and then, because Jake still wasn't home from the Blairs', he sneaked in a few more minutes of television. It wasn't long before Jake returned.

"Bed now, Scott," he said.

"What were you talking to the Blairs about for so long?" Scott asked.

"Oh, things," Jake answered. "Come on, Scotty, off you go. I'll tell you all about it in the morning."

"Night then," Scott said.

As Scott turned to go to his room, Jake put a hand on his shoulder and stopped him. He looked at him intently, a long, deep look. "You're a good kid, Scotty," he said. And then he drew Scott to him and held him for a short moment, very closely.

Scott went to bed, happy at Jake's show of affection, but also faintly puzzled.

In the morning over breakfast, Jake put down his coffee mug and, resting his elbows on the table and his chin in his hands, said, "Scotty, do you know how old I am?"

Scott looked at him in surprise.

"I never really thought about it," he said truthfully, for indeed he hadn't. Jake seemed a person who had always been there and would always be there, stomping around among the trees in his red checkered shirt. "About sixty?"

"I'll soon be sixty-five," Jake said. "I'm getting on."

"Jeremiah says he's a hundred and two. Is that true?"

"No, it's not. Jeremiah is eighty-five. But we're all getting older around here."

Scott chewed on his toast, feeling uncomfortable. "I guess we *all* have to get older," he said.

"Of course, but that's not the point," Jake said. "The point is, I don't know how long I'll be able to go on looking after you."

Anxiety flooded Scott. "Why, Jake? Are you sick?" He thought of the times Jake had complained about the bursitis in his shoulder.

"No, no," Jake laughed, "I'm well and hearty. But no one goes on forever."

"But I'll be grown up soon, you don't have to worry. I'll be grown up in two or three years."

"No, you won't be, Scott. Not for much longer than that. And you'll be needing all kinds of things I won't be able to give you. Even right now Mr. Blair thinks you should be having art lessons."

"Art lessons!" Scott cried. Ah yes, he had overheard that suggestion. "I don't need art lessons," he continued. "I do just fine by myself. I have fun. I don't plan to become some great artist."

"Mr. Blair thinks you could be one."

"Oh, Mr. Blair! Jake, you pay too much attention to what the Blairs say. We got along perfectly well before they came."

"Scott," Jake said, watching Scott carefully and speaking gently, "the Blairs have taken a great liking to you. They think you're a fine lad and very smart into the bargain. They want to see that you have every chance in life."

Scott stared at Jake. Jake was trying to tell him something. Once again Scott was filled with anxiety. "What d'you mean, Jake?" he asked hoarsely.

"Well, Scotty-boy, the Blairs have been talking to me about you — quite a lot. And the more I think about what they say, the more sense it makes. It's true, Scotty, that they could give you everything you will ever need in life, and love into the bargain. They've grown fond of you, Scotty. Very fond."

"What do you mean, Jake? What do you mean?" Scott repeated. His piece of toast fell from his hand to his plate. Stark fear showed in his eyes; his face became drawn.

"I mean that the Blairs want you to live with them in the States, Scott."

An early morning wind rippled through the trees, chasing up the clouds; the sunlight disappeared. Silence hung in the kitchen like a dead bird caught in a tree.

"You must be crazy, Jake," Scott said at last.

"No. I'm not. I said something like that to the Blairs, too, when they first suggested it. But, as I say, the more I think about it, the more sense it makes. Look, Scotty-boy, I'm getting old. Let's face it, I could *die* any day. What would you do then? I took you in when you were little because your dad and mom were my best friends and there weren't any relatives. But my time is growing short — my useful years — and here are the Blairs, still quite young, tremendously wealthy, ready to do everything for you. They want to adopt you finally, to bring you up as their own son. We can't turn down such a chance, Scotty. You do see that, don't you?"

But Scott had pushed back his chair and stumbled out of the kitchen to his own room, where he threw himself down on his bed, sobbing bitterly.

Jake followed him and sat down on the edge of the bed. "I thought you liked the Blairs. I thought you liked them a lot."

"Of course I do!" Scott gulped through his tears. "Oh, I *do* like them, Jake. But not to live with. Not to leave *you*!"

"Come on now, Scotty," Jake said. "Be reasonable. How can we refuse such an offer? What can I give you except a hard life and the company of Pete Boggle and Sammy Gore? Mrs. Blair's right; my friends aren't that good for you, son. And if your mother were alive, she'd probably agree with Mrs. Blair."

"I *like* your friends, I don't *care* what Mrs. Blair says. I'm not going to leave Twin Rivers. Not ever. Not ever, ever, ever. Even if I never have any money as long as I live. This is my home and I'm staying here." Scott's words came out muffled, for his face was buried in his pillow, but they sounded very determined.

Jake got up. "I'll leave you to think about it, Scotty-boy. It isn't such a bad idea as it seems at first. I didn't like it right away, either. But it does make sense."

Jake left the house, and Scott lay very still. So Granny McKay had been right after all, and Dan too. The Blairs had come from the coast, and, ocean spirits or not, they were trying to break up Scott's home. Well, let them try. Scott banged his fist down on his pillow. See if they could succeed. Leave Jake and Dan and Gran and Jeremiah — and Flappy too, probably — what an idea! And leave Canada! If he went to live in the United States with the Blairs as their adopted son he would become an American. But he was Canadian! He couldn't ever be anything else.

Scott didn't see the Blairs that day. They had gone off to visit Banff and Lake Louise for a few days.

80

Scott found Dan and, with a huge lump in his throat, told him the whole story. In spite of himself, tears ran down his face as he talked.

"Gran was right," Dan said, awe-stricken. "They *are* ocean spirits, or at least they're being used by them. They're trying to steal you away from the river."

"You didn't believe your gran when she first warned me," Scott reminded him again.

"I know. But grans are quite often right," Daniel said, smiling sadly. After a while he said, "I guess you'll have to go."

"I'll never go," Scott said. "Never."

"There's nothing you can do. If Jake thinks it's a good idea, what can you do?"

Dan's words echoed dully on the summer air.

Scott stopped crying. He dried his eyes with his sleeve, leaving smudges across his face. Dan was right. Protesting wasn't going to do any good. A feeling of flat helplessness spread through his body to every limb, an unwelcome realization that if the grown-ups around him thought something was for his good, then they would bring it about, whether he fought against it or not. Crying wasn't going to do any good. Nothing was going to do any good. He was only a boy after all. What could he do if all the grown-ups were against him? All the grown-ups, even Jake. That really hurt!

Scott went to bed that night without saying good night to Jake — which hurt more than anything else. But Jake came into Scott's room and pushed him around on his bed, as he used to do when Scott was younger.

"Snap out of it," he said to Scott, "please. It isn't the end of the world. All the Blairs are asking is for you to give it a try. It won't hurt you to go and live with them for a while. It's not even that far — only Seattle."

That's not the point, Scott cried, deep inside himself. It didn't matter *where* it was. It wasn't Twin Rivers, and it wasn't with Jake and Dan and Gran. Could it be that Jake didn't care? Once Scott went, the Blairs would never let him go. Why couldn't Jake see that? They would force him to do as they wanted because they were older and stronger, and thought they were wiser. They would make him feel guilty because they were doing so much for him. The flat, helpless feeling filled Scott again.

"How can you give me away, just like that?" he cried to Jake. "You've only known these people for a few weeks. How d'you know what they'll do with me? How do you know anything?"

"I do know quite a lot," Jake replied quietly. "Mr. Blair is a very well-thought-of business man. They are the very finest people you could find. There's no doubt about that. And they certainly have taken to you, Scotty. Otherwise, why would they propose such a thing? There are many other boys they could take into their home. But it's *you* they want. Something happens between people sometimes; you get that feeling that someone's special."

"Well, I wish they hadn't got that feeling about me," Scott wailed. "You're the person who's special to me, and I thought you loved me, Jake. How can you think of sending me away?"

Jake put his arms around Scott and held him tight.

"I do love you, Scotty, that's why I must persuade you to do this. Can't you understand? I can't stand between you and such good fortune. I love you too much."

Scott's skinny arms were tight around Jake's neck and his suntanned face pressed close to Jake's sandpapery cheek. As they clung together, Scott felt a warm tear creep down between their faces. And it wasn't *his* tear, because he had used up all his tears for that day.

Chapter 11

Dark Days and Danger

When the Blairs got back from their trip to Banff and Lake Louise, Scott managed to avoid them quite successfully for a while. He and Dan hid in the woods and down by the river, and one day they took a trip to Boston Bar on the bus and stayed there all day. But when they came home for supper that evening, Mrs. Blair came out of her cabin as they were passing by.

"Scott," she said, smiling, "I do want to talk to you, dear. Would you stop by after supper? I'll be waiting for you."

I'll be busy, Scott wanted to say. I don't want to talk to you, or see you again, ever. But he was afraid to say anything like that.

"All right," he mumbled, and after dinner he walked slowly across to Mrs. Blair's cottage. Mrs. Blair was sitting outside.

"Sit down, dear," she said. "We've got so much to talk about. I know Jake's told you about our idea, and I know you're upset about it. I can certainly understand that. But you know, we don't have to make any final decisions right away."

Mrs. Blair smiled at Scott a little sadly. She must be disappointed, he thought. Had she really expected him to respond to her plan with enthusiasm?

"Mr. Blair and I have grown awfully fond of you, Scott," she said, a bit shyly.

Scott had sat down on the grass, and he pulled out a tuft and started to shred it. "I like you lots, too," he said gruffly.

"I know it's hard to make changes," Mrs. Blair said, "but life is full of changes." Scott didn't answer or look at her. "Mr. Blair and I have many things and lots of money, Scott, but we've never had a child. You see, I lost a baby long ago and couldn't have another."

There was a short silence. "Why. . . why didn't you adopt one then?" Scott asked.

"I don't really know why. We did think about it, but I was afraid I couldn't love a child enough if it wasn't my very own. I suppose that was because I had just lost my own baby. Or maybe I was just afraid to take the responsibility. I'm really a coward, you know, Scott. And James would love to have children in our home."

Scott tore up another tuft of grass.

"I don't want to let this chance go by because of being afraid to ask you," she said.

Scott looked up. Her brown eyes wrapped him up, warmly and completely. It had never occurred to him that it would be hard for Mrs. Blair to make the suggestion. Now, through his own distress, Scott saw that Mrs. Blair was good and kind, and also a bit scared. She had opened her heart to him and was shyly inviting him to enter. But he didn't want to go in, at least not all the way.

"I'm — I'm glad you want me to live with you, Mrs. Blair," he said, "but — it's just that Jake. . . I can't leave Jake."

"I know about Jake. I've become very, very fond of him myself, and Mr. Blair thinks the world of him. You wouldn't be saying good-bye to Jake forever! You could visit often. And you'd see Dan and Mrs. McKay, too. There would be nothing to prevent you."

Except that it wouldn't work out that way, Scott thought. Except that, once I got settled there, all kinds of things would come up to prevent me.

He shook his head.

"Scott, you know you have a great deal of artistic talent. I'm not praising you to get my way. It's simply true. But talent isn't enough. Talent needs training and opportunity. Dear as Jake is, he isn't able to give you those advantages."

"I don't want advantages," Scott mumbled. "I'm happy just doing my own thing in my own way."

"You are, right now. But later you'll come to regret it, to resent that you didn't have the chance to get a fine education and art training. We would like to give you that chance."

Scott nodded. He dropped his eyes again. It was hard to look into those sincere brown eyes and say no. "I do understand, Mrs. Blair," he said in a low voice. "Thanks, thanks a whole lot, only. . ." and he shook his head again.

"There's just one more thing I'd like to say," Mrs. Blair said. "And again I'm not using this as some sort of blackmail." She laughed a little. "But Scott, you should think of Jake. He's not getting any younger. He loves you very dearly and it must be a great worry to him to know that he's not able to give you all the things he would like you to have. He must often wonder what would become of you if he ever became ill, or if he was suddenly no longer around to give you love and advice."

Scott sat in silent misery. If only he knew what would be best for Jake's sake. If his going would really make things easier for Jake, he might have to consider the idea. But that would be the *only* reason he would even think about it.

Mrs. Blair didn't try to press her advantage. They sat in silence.

"Why don't you just think about it?" Mrs. Blair said, at last. "We're fond of each other, Scott. We could make a good thing of this."

Scott dared to look up again into the brown eyes. "Okay, I'll think about it. But don't be mad if I don't come."

"Of course I won't be mad," Mrs. Blair said. "I'll like you just as much. Always. I won't be mad. A bit sad of course, but never mad."

Scott got to his feet. "I'll think about it," he repeated. Then he walked away, his head bent, his lower lip caught between his teeth.

Though Scott continued to struggle, like the helpless little fish he and Dan sometimes caught in their nets, deep inside himself he knew that he had lost the battle. From every point of view, going with the Blairs seemed the sensible thing to do. Except for the hurting. Scott was not sure that he could stand the hurting.

Jake did not say much during the next few days. Nobody said much. Granny McKay found herself very busy with a large order of weaving, and when Scott saw her, it was impossible to read her eyes.

"What do *you* think, Gran?" Scott asked once.

And she replied, "I can't argue against it. If it's opportunity you want, few things could be better."

Was it opportunity he wanted? What *did* he want? And what was "opportunity," anyway? He never seemed to be able to talk to Dan these days because Dan was always watching TV, even shows that Scott knew he didn't care for. When you're watching TV, you don't have to talk. Obviously Dan didn't want to talk.

A darkness settled upon Scott. Even the weather seemed in sympathy, for it turned stormy, and black clouds banked around the mountain tops every day. It was hot and heavy, just like the weight on Scott's mind. What was his decision to be?

Often Scott took the mask down from its place on the wall, and, sitting on his bed, he would study it carefully. The strange face looked back at him. Sometimes it seemed to Scott that there were eyes behind the cavities, wise eyes. He would sit very still trying to hold on to the illusion.

"What should I do?" he would ask the mask again and again, half believing that the old magic would work, that the mask would speak to him. But it lay silently in his hands. Yet somehow it comforted him. It felt good to hold it.

Scott hadn't had a talk with Mr. Blair for a long time. They waved when they saw each other and spoke if they met, but they didn't stop to chat. But one evening, when Mr. Blair was getting a large painting out of his car, he asked Scott to help him. Carefully they lifted the painting out and took it into the cabin. Mrs. Blair was out, making a telephone call from the motel office.

Scott was admiring Mr. Blair's painting when the painter turned to him and said, "Okay Scott, old fellow, I haven't said much, but our idea isn't half bad, you know. I always think that I could be painting twice as well if I'd had a chance when I was a kid. Maybe I'm fooling myself, but there's lots of resentment in me that I wish I didn't have. Maybe you'll never feel like this, but, Scott, it's no fun. Why don't you give our idea a try? No harm in giving things a try. Right?"

Now he had someone else's arguments to consider. Scott felt that he could read everyone's feelings, but he knew the decision had to be his. And yet it would never truly be his decision; he felt it would be forced on him.

"If I go, I could come back at Christmas," he said to Dan the next day when Scott managed to drag him out for a walk.

But Dan shook his head. "That's the time they'll want you with them most. That's the family-making time."

"Then you could come to Seattle. They'd ask you."

"And leave Gran at Christmas? Not likely. It won't work, Scott."

"Then in the spring," Scott said, his voice a little unsteady. "I could come back at Easter."

"They won't let you," Dan said. "Don't you see? They'll want you to forget everything here. They'll want you to become an American and love their country the way you love everything here."

During the week there was a letter for Jake. His sister was worse and had to be placed in a special nursing home. It would cost more money. That evening, when Jake pulled out the lawn mower, he cringed suddenly and clutched his shoulder. "It's nothing. Just that old bursitis acting up," he said as Scott ran up in concern.

"Let me mow the lawn," Scott cried, but Jake waved him off.

But it set Scott thinking. Mrs. Blair was right and Jake was right. People got old, and one of these days Jake would need care instead of always giving it. Who would give him that care? That was another reason he should stay — he could look after Jake. But probably Jake wouldn't agree to that. For a while Scott avoided everyone. He had to get things straight in his head.

Dan, too, was having a bad time. True, he had no decision to make but he understood how hard it was for Scott to make this one. The boys were so close, Dan could feel what Scott was feeling, but he couldn't help. It had to be Scott's decision. The result of that decision would affect him more than he cared to think about.

One evening Dan went down to the river. He hadn't gone there lately with Scott, because going down to the river meant talking a lot, and Dan didn't want to talk. Now he sat on a rock dangling his legs.

Suddenly Mrs. Blair appeared at the top of the river bank a little farther down. The bank rose steeply at that point and gave a fine view of the river tumbling away over the rocks.

Daniel watched Mrs. Blair. He knew that she was standing on a dangerous spot. The bank beneath her was eroded and might give way. Dan had noticed it yesterday and had meant to tell someone. He knew he should warn Mrs. Blair now, but he didn't want to. He hated her. Let her fall in, he felt more than thought. She was the person who was causing everyone so much misery. Dan remembered Scott saying that Mrs. Blair couldn't swim. If she drowned, Scott would never have to go away.

But, even as all these thoughts passed through his head, Daniel knew they were rubbish. A person didn't just stand by and let someone fall to her death, no matter what.

Dan leaped to his feet, calling, "Be careful, Mrs. Blair. Keep away. Go back."

But Mrs. Blair didn't seem to hear him. She smiled and nodded and waved to Dan.

"Be careful," Dan yelled again. "Keep away!"

He gestured wildly, trying to make himself clear. Mrs. Blair made signs to indicate that she couldn't hear him, and, in order to catch his words, she moved closer to the dangerous edge.

The next moment the earth beneath her feet began to crumble. Mrs. Blair screamed and swayed, clutching at nothing. Then the whole bank on which she stood slipped away down the cliff into the river, carrying her with it.

There was no time for anything but the fastest action. Dan scrambled down the rocks and dived, a long thin streak of muscle and brown skin. The river was turbulent at that spot, a place that he and Scott would never have chosen for a swim. Mrs. Blair had panicked and was floundering and screaming, trying to grasp at the slippery rocks.

In a few strokes Dan was beside the desperate woman. He knew where there was a shallow place, if only he could get her to it. Battling the swirling water and the flailing Mrs. Blair, Dan yelled instructions in her ear. To his relief, she did as she was told, and together they found the shallow spot where they could both stand up, hanging on to each other and a jagged rock. Then Dan hollered for help.

Soon there were many volunteers rushing to help. Mrs. Blair was exhausted but otherwise fine and refused to go to the hospital. She was taken back to Twin Rivers and put to bed, where she kept repeating that Daniel had saved her life.

But Dan was nowhere to be found. He had run away in all the excitement. Even Scott couldn't find him.

Much later in the evening, Mr. Blair tramped up to the house in the woods and knocked on Granny McKay's door. Dan opened it.

"Dan," Mr. Blair said, "where did you go? We looked and looked. We're so grateful to you. Mrs. Blair would like to talk to you, to thank you."

"I don't want to talk to Mrs. Blair," Dan said, his eyes downcast.

"But you saved her life!"

"She was drowning. Anyone would have done it." Dan investigated a crack in the floor with his toe.

"Dan," Mr. Blair said, "I know how you feel about us, and I'm sorry. But if you truly love Scott, if he's your dear friend, you must try to see that our plans for him make lots of sense."

Dan still said nothing. Mr. Blair searched in his pocket and brought out some money.

"Mrs. Blair and I plan to do much more than this for your grandmother and you, but take this, just as a start, from two very, very grateful people. I'm sure you could have some fun with it."

He put the money into Dan's hand and turned swiftly to walk back down the path.

Dan glanced at the money. Then, with a half-sob, he raced down the pathway after Mr. Blair. Stuffing the notes into one of Mr. Blair's pockets, he turned and dashed back to his house, banging the door behind him. He wasn't going to take their old money! Maybe they could buy Scott—but not him, Daniel. And not his Grandmother either!

Chapter 12

Bellevue

Gradually Scott began to understand that no matter how he felt about it, the overwhelming weight of opinion was that he should go with the Blairs. Seeing Jake nursing his bursitis and worrying about his sister gave Scott the final push.

"You do want me to go, don't you?" he said to Jake.

And Jake answered, "It makes sense, Scotty. Don't make it hard for me."

"Okay, Jake," Scott said, his heart as heavy as a bag of nails and just as cold. "I won't make it hard for you. But you'll come — often — won't you? And I'll come here for holidays."

"You seem to think we'll never see each other again. Seattle isn't the other side of the world, Scotty. It isn't out in space somewhere." To Scott it seemed that it was, and in a sense he knew he was right.

All too soon the day came when he had to say good-bye. The Blairs thought that if they left in mid-August it would give Scott time to get used to his new home and to get to know some of the young people before school started.

Scott went to see Dan and Granny McKay. He would have preferred to go away without any leave-taking, but at the last moment he couldn't go without seeing them.

Granny knew better than to shed tears. "Make sure you write," she said. "We'll look forward to your letters, and we'll write too."

"Of course, Gran," he said, "of course. I'll write about every single thing."

"And Scott, another thing," Granny McKay said. "That mask. Take good care of it, won't you?"

"But of course, Gran," Scott said again. "It will *always* be my favorite thing."

"It's strange about old things," Granny said. "They seem to communicate a special feeling. Sometimes it's a good feeling, sometimes not. That old mask gives me a good feeling — the way our river does."

"I know," Scott said. "It gives me one, too." He hugged Granny tightly. "I'll never part with it," he said. "Never."

Annie McKay held Scott away from her, her hands on his shoulders, and looked deep into his eyes. "If you ever want to know right from wrong," she said, "the mask will tell you. I can't tell you how, but I'm sure it will."

"I'll trust it," Scott said, blinking hard. With a little nod, Annie released him.

Scott looked at Dan. Dan was still in his pyjamas, standing, feet crossed, leaning against the kitchen door.

"See you, Dan," Scott said.

"Sure," Dan replied.

Scott said good-bye to everyone privately and begged everyone not to come out to the car, especially Jake. He couldn't bear even the thought of waving good-bye to Jake.

So nobody came to watch that morning as the car, carrying Scott and the Blairs, moved slowly down the narrow road that led to the Trans-Canada highway. Only Flappy ran round in circles, barking anxiously, and then sat down in the middle of the roadway.

"If only I could have had Flappy with me, it would have helped," Scott wept within himself.

But Mrs. Blair had decided against taking the dog. "Flappy will be happier here at home than in the city," she had said. "We'll get you a dog in Seattle, Scott. Friends of ours have a lab; she's expecting puppies."

Scott was wearing his best clothes, the outfit that Jake had bought him when they went to Vancouver. Mrs. Blair had looked at them and said that they would do until they got home. "Then we'll go on a shopping spree," she said, her eyes full of smiles.

Scott knew that she was trying to cheer him up. But he just felt angry and resentful. Jake had gone without things to give Scott his trip *and* buy him these great clothes. Why did Mrs. Blair make him feel they weren't good enough?

Scott and the Blairs stopped overnight in Vancouver, as Mr. Blair had to visit Canadian and American officials to find out about Scott's entry into the United States. Scott heard him discussing the matter later with Mrs. Blair. They talked about visiting visas and adoption papers, but Scott purposely shut his ears. He didn't want to hear anything about those things.

They paid a visit to the Taylors and the Blacks, who exclaimed about how thrilled Scott must be at the idea of going to the States. Scott just felt miserable and had to force himself to smile. He was glad when the visit was over. But as they were leaving, Sandy Black squeezed his shoulder, and when Scott looked up at him, his lips tight, Sandy made a wry little grimace. Scott knew that Sandy understood.

In the morning they drove through Vancouver on their way to the freeway to the United States. Yes, it was the same Vancouver, but how different from a few weeks ago the city seemed to Scott. Then it had been an exciting and wonderful place, and Scott had felt that it belonged to him. Now it was only a place in which to say good-bye. Soon it would no longer have anything to do with him.

The car left the Oak Street Bridge and sped on toward the George Massey tunnel under the south arm of the Fraser River. On the last stretch of Canadian highway, Scott looked back at the city behind him and made a secret pact. He would come back. He didn't know when, but someday he would come back.

When they came to the Peace Arch and drove across the border, after a brief stop at the Customs office, Scott felt as though huge gates — the gates to Canada — had clanged behind him.

The drive to Bellevue took between two and three hours. Scott sat in the back seat, answering questions, but he didn't feel much like talking and was glad when Mrs. Blair put on the radio. On and on they drove, past Mount Vernon and Marysville and Everett, but the names held no magic like the place names on Vancouver Island. At last they left the freeway and entered Bellevue.

"We're almost home," Mrs. Blair said.

"Home," Scott thought, "home!"

They drove through the attractive city, and in spite of himself Scott began to feel the stirrings of interest. After all, *he* had agreed to come with the Blairs, so he supposed he should at least make an effort.

He could not hold back his admiration when they drove up to the Blairs' home on the shore of Lake Washington. It was a large, rambling house that managed to look homey and welcoming in spite of its size.

"What gorgeous flowers!" Scott exclaimed when he saw the beds. "And what a lot of lawn to have to cut!" But what suddenly comforted Scott and cheered him were the trees — lots of trees, and big trees. "There's no river here," thought Scott, "but at least I still have trees — and a lake."

Scott walked with the Blairs through the carpeted hallway, past an elegant living room, and up the stairway to a room done in blues and greens, which looked out on Lake Washington.

"This will be your room," Mrs. Blair told him. "At the moment it's just an extra guest room, but we'll change it round whichever way you want, and you can have whatever you like in it."

"Thank you," Scott said, "but I like it the way it is. It's neat."

"And of course there's the rec room downstairs where you'll be able to bring your friends."

Mr. Blair took Scott on a tour of the house while Mrs. Blair went to get lunch. There were four bedrooms upstairs and a sombre study lined with bookshelves. Mr. Blair stopped briefly in the study to put Scott's papers in one of his desk drawers. Scott said nothing; he seemed to have a catch in his throat.

Downstairs there was a very grand living room, all in white and gold, a dining room with a crystal chandelier, and a kitchen with every kind of modern appliance — most of which Scott had only seen on TV. There was also a studio with a huge window where Mr. Blair did his painting.

Mr. Blair and Scott brought in the luggage, then they had a late lunch. As soon as he could, Scott went outside to explore.

The Blair home and all the surrounding houses were set in landscaped grounds that sloped down to the shore of Lake Washington.

Two boys next door were trying to drag a huge piece of driftwood ashore. It was heavy, and they were having trouble. Scott rolled up his pant-legs and joined them in the water. Scott's sinewy strength was just what was needed to move the log. With whoops of triumph, the boys hauled it up on shore.

"Gee, thanks," a fair-haired boy said to Scott, grinning, as he wiped his dirty face with a sleeve. "Are you visiting the Blairs?"

Scott nodded. "I'm Scott Anderson," he said.

"I'm Tom Kelly, and he's Greg Rolston. I live there," indicating the house next to the Blairs, "and Greg lives a few houses down. You going to stay long?"

Scott's heart contracted painfully. "For a while," he replied.

"Just for the rest of the summer?"

"No, I'm going to go to school here."

"Great. We're all going to the new school. It's just finished. Are you a relative of the Blairs?" Greg Rolston, who asked the question, had black, curly hair and a laughing face.

"No, they're just . . . friends," Scott said, hesitantly.

"Your folks away someplace?"

"No," said Scott. "I'm the one who's away. I'm a Canadian and I live with Jake O'Burn in the Fraser Canyon. Jake's my guardian because my parents are dead. I'm just staying with the Blairs now because they thought — maybe I'd like it better here."

"And do you?" asked Tom eagerly.

"I don't know yet," Scott hedged. "I just came."

"The Blairs have a yacht, did you know? A big one. Boy, you're lucky."

"Dan and I made a canoe once," Scott said. "It was a good canoe, and we took it into the river down some rapids and smashed it. Jake blew his top. He almost belted us he was so mad. He said we could have killed ourselves. The rapids seemed small, but the river's sure strong."

"Who's Dan?"

"My best friend."

"Jim Crawley would like to hear that story," Tom laughed.

"Why? Who's Jim Crawley?"

Tom shook his head. "He's a real crazy kid. A friend of ours, sort of. He likes doing wild things. He borrowed his cousin's sports car once and drove it."

"And he's tops in sports," Greg added, "everything — football, baseball, swimming — you name it, and Jim Crawley's the best."

"Yeah, well, you'll meet Jim when he gets back from vacation," Tom said. He shrugged and turned back to the log. "We thought we could make something out of this, sort of hollow it out somehow."

"That wouldn't be too hard," Scott nodded. "I'll help you if you like."

"That would be great," Greg said. "We don't know much about canoes and things like that."

The three boys sat down on the ground and stared out over the lake. "Hey," Tom exclaimed, springing up and picking something up from among the pebbles, "a piece of obsidian. That's hard to find."

"This isn't obsidian," Scott said, examining the find.

"It's black slate. I'll give you a piece of obsidian if you like. I brought my rock collection."

"You've got a collection! Can we see it?"

"Sure."

The boys returned to the Blair house. Nobody was around. "Come up to my room," Scott invited them. "My room," thought Scott. It had even seemed natural to say it.

Up in his bedroom Scott brought out his precious rocks, which he had packed carefully in a carton, and laid them on the soft carpet, one by one.

"You've got some good stuff here," Tom said. "This is a great collection."

"Hey, what's this?" Greg cried.

In another carton, carefully wrapped in paper, Scott had packed the mask Dan had given him.

"It's my mask," Scott said. "It's an Indian mask. Dan gave it to me and it makes us brothers."

"Dan? The guy you went in the canoe with?"

"Yep."

"Are you really his brother?"

"Not his blood brother. But when he gave me the mask that made us brothers. It was in his family."

"Gee, that sounds neat," Tom said. "Do you *feel* that you're his brother?"

"Yes, I do," Scott said. To his deep embarrassment his eyes filled with tears and his chest became so full that he couldn't breathe. But nobody saw, the boys were too interested in the mask and the rocks.

That evening, after supper, Scott went up to his room and took down a picture that was hanging on the wall over the bureau and hung up the mask in its place. In this way he would see it every day just before he fell asleep. It would be a link between him and Dan.

Mrs. Blair came up after him to see that he had unpacked properly and that he had everything he needed. "There's your mask," she exclaimed. "It looks pretty impressive, doesn't it?"

"I thought you wouldn't mind if I hung it there."

"You can do whatever you like in your room. Of course."

"I took down that picture," Scott said, feeling guilty. "Maybe we could hang it someplace else."

"Sure, we'll think about it tomorrow. Before you go to bed, come down and have some milk and cookies if you like. You could watch TV for a while, or do whatever you like. This is your home, Scott."

"Thank you," Scott said. When Mrs. Blair was so kind, how was it that he suddenly felt so unbearably miserable again?

Chapter 13

A New Life

Scott's new friends came to call on him every day, and the last days of the holidays passed like the flipped pages of a scrap book. Every day there was something new to see and do.

Mr. Blair took Scott and his friends sailing, and Scott learned how to hoist and position sails, how to anchor, how to dock, and how not to fall off the boat when it tipped in the wind and waves. With the sun and the sea-spray on his body, and his head full of newly-learned skills, Twin Rivers faded from Scott's thoughts for hours at a time. In between instructions on handling and safety, Mr. Blair told the boys tales of the sea, often sad and mysterious, and then Scott would be reminded of Granny McKay's ocean spirits.

Once or twice Mr. Blair said to Scott, always privately, something like, "Beginning to enjoy things a bit again, maybe?" And Scott would grin, although he always felt a little pang inside.

Soon after his arrival in Bellevue, Mrs. Blair said to Scott, "I know you wouldn't be comfortable calling us Mom and Dad, but we've gone beyond the Mr. and Mrs. stage, don't you think? What about Aunt Amelia and Uncle James?" And Scott had agreed.

Mr. Blair was going back to work at the end of the month, and before he went, he offered to take Scott and Mrs. Blair to lunch up in the Space Needle. "Could Tom and Greg come too?" Scott asked, and Tom and Greg were invited.

It was fun at the top of the structure, which towered over the city and the surrounding countryside. They sat at a table and looked out at space, while the restaurant slowly revolved, constantly opening new vistas. Scott was now familiar with menus and quite enjoyed ordering.

"This is a small celebration for Scott," Mrs. Blair said, "to wish him luck in his new school," and they all ordered desserts with huge gobs of cream in his honor. After lunch, they walked around outdoors on the observation deck.

For a brief moment, while Tom and Greg and Mrs. Blair were a short distance away arguing about a building on the landscape below, Mr. Blair said to Scott, "It's not going too badly, is it?"

And Scott smiled and said, "Not too badly."

At home, or what he now called home, things gradually began to change. At first there were just helpful hints — how to eat peas so that they didn't keep escaping from his fork, how not to slurp when eating soup, how to pull sheets and blankets straight so that his bed didn't have funny lumps in it. And then a few rules were added to the hints. Bedtime was at ten, not five or ten after, and meals were served on time — if you were late, you missed the meal. This was hard, because meals had been so haphazard with Jake. Television was limited to certain programs and times.

"There are so many channels here," Mrs. Blair said, "and there's a lot of rubbish on them. You don't want to

103

waste your time watching rubbish, do you?" Unfortunately what Mrs. Blair called rubbish was exactly what Scott was dying to watch, but he didn't argue. He got around it by spending time with Greg, whose mother wasn't so particular. But he felt guilty about it.

School started. On the first morning, Scott walked to school with Tom Kelly and Greg Rolston. They had already visited the new school and viewed it from the grounds and pronounced it "super." The interior was handsome. There were panelled corridors, a glittering cafeteria, a high-ceilinged gym, a large auditorium. The boys were impressed.

And Scott met Jim Crawley. Greg and Tom had spoken of Jim that first day by the lakeshore, and since then, Scott had often heard Jim's name mentioned by other boys. Jim was an ace swimmer, a pitcher on the baseball team, a good football player. The boys obviously admired him. But it seemed to Scott that their admiration was mixed with something else, although he wasn't too sure what it was. He was soon to find out.

At the end of the first day, Tom, Greg, and Scott were about to take the narrow, tree-lined path leading to a side street near their homes when three boys barred their way.

"Hi, Crawley," Tom Kelly said to the tallest and sturdiest of the three. "You back at last, eh?"

"'Taint my ghost," Crawley replied, half smiling but not moving away. "You the new guy?" he continued, staring at Scott.

Scott stared back at Crawley. "I'm new in Bellevue," he said, "but I guess everybody's new at this school."

Crawley grinned. "A joker yet! You're the Canuck, aren't you?"

"So?" Tom Kelly bridled.

104

"Keep out of this, Kelly," Crawley said. "I bet this kid can take care of himself. You visiting here?"

"Wish I were."

"What do you mean?"

"I mean that Bellevue is a nice place to visit," said Scott, noncommitally.

"Hmmm." Crawley surveyed Scott with interest. "I hear you're quite a swimmer," he said, changing the subject.

"I enjoy swimming."

"Where did you practise back home? In a mud hole?"

The color began to creep up Scott's neck, but he kept his head. "Is that what *you* do?" he asked.

Crawley studied Scott again in silence while the other boys fidgetted. "You know something, kid?" he said. "I like you."

Scott stared back at Crawley and finally started to pass him.

"Say 'please,' " Crawley taunted him, his eyes watching.

Scott continued to move closer to the edge of the path.

Suddenly Crawley caught his shirt front in his muscular hand and pushed Scott back, his eyes still oddly watchful.

Then the anger that Scott had been holding back burst loose. Two quick movements, and Crawley was on his back. Scott's whole body tensed, his fist readied for Crawley's comeback. Scott was slim and not too tall; he seemed frail, but his muscles were like knots beneath his shirt. He stood and waited — but nothing happened.

Crawley propped himself up on his elbows on the grass — and laughed!

For a minute, the other boys stared at the two antagonists. Then they began to laugh with Crawley.

"I *said* I liked you, kid," Crawley said. "You have no idea what you just did. You knocked down the invincible Crawley. You've got guts. I should get up and pummel you to a pulp."

"Well, why don't you try?" Scott's breath was coming in short gasps, and he was not laughing.

Crawley shook with mirth. "I don't want to fight you. You don't deserve a beating, Canuck. Besides, I'm scared of you — no kidding!"

"You're nuts," Scott said. But suddenly he relaxed; then he, too, laughed. And that was the beginning of his friendship with Jim Crawley.

In Scott, Jim Crawley found a willing companion. There was nothing Jim did that Scott was afraid to do, and Scott added many ideas of his own. Although he stayed good friends with Tom and Greg, he was drawn more and more to Jim Crawley. Jim provided a special excitement and challenge, just what Scott seemed to need to keep his mind off Twin Rivers.

Each day, as soon as school was over, Jim Crawley would be waiting for Scott at the school door. They would report home and then dash off together for a couple of hours of fun before supper and homework.

Their amusements were various. "Let's make stilts," Jim Crawley suggested one day, and they made them and fooled around on them until Jim fell on the cement and sprained his wrist. That settled the stilts.

When Jim was better, he wanted new roller skates, and Scott got some too. On the skates they whizzed around the walks and neighborhood until Scott fell into Mr. Crawley's prize chrysanthemums. For a while the roller skates were confiscated.

"I'm awfully sorry about the flowers, but it was only an accident," Scott pleaded with Mrs. Blair. But she was adamant. Mr. Crawley was angry, and he was a neighbor. You had to live with your neighbors, she said, and the least Scott could do was to stay off his skates for a while.

Let's race our bikes downhill," Scott suggested another day. "Let's see who can get farthest without holding the handlebars."

They did that, and had the bad luck of meeting Mrs. Crawley, who was out for a stroll with a friend. Mrs. Crawley wanted to put a stop to Jim playing with that wild Scott Anderson before he got killed, but Jim got around her and promised to take it easy.

"We'd better do something quiet for a bit," he said to Scott. "Mom's really cracking down."

"All right," Scott agreed. "Let's build a look-out. A platform up in that old tree. We could see way over the lake, right to Seattle."

"Neat idea," Jim said.

"I'll ask Uncle James where we can get some wood," Scott said.

"It's not going to be easy," Mr. Blair said, staring up at the tree and rubbing his chin. "Kind of tricky, fitting in the planks, but we'll try. We mustn't hurt the tree, you know." It turned out that Mr. Blair knew someone who had spare planks left over from a building project.

"Have you ever made a look-out platform before?" Jim asked Scott.

"Once. I made one with Dan. But it wasn't very good, sort of wobbly. Jake didn't think much of it. It collapsed finally."

"Dan was your best friend, eh?"

"He still is," Scott said.

"It must have been fun living by the Canyon."

"Lots of fun," Scott said, hammering hard.

"Tell me more about it," Jim Crawley said.

Scott took a while measuring the next piece of wood with his tape before he answered.

"I've told you lots. What else do you want to know?"

"You haven't told me that much. You didn't tell me what your school was like."

"Smallish. Nothing like ours. But it felt...like it belonged to me."

Crawley looked at Scott. He thought he'd heard a tiny break in Scott's voice.

"Did your friend go to the same school?"

"Of course. We did everything together. He lived near us. His Gran helped with our motel. I told you."

"Must've been fun, living in a motel. What was it like?"

"Okay, I guess. I've told you, it belonged to Jake. He was my guardian."

"Isn't he your guardian any more?"

"Yes, he is. But the Blairs want to adopt me."

"Then you'll become an American."

"I know," Scott said in a husky voice, bending over his work.

"Don't you want to?"

"Not really."

"Why not?"

"Because it wouldn't be true."

"What wouldn't?"

"Being an American. It wouldn't be true because I'm a Canadian. I feel Canadian. A paper won't make any difference."

"I think I know what you mean. But it won't be bad — America's great. But tell me more about Canada."

109

So Scott told Jim about the places he had been to and the places he had only heard about but where he planned to go some day. He got carried away and talked a lot, and then stopped and laughed at himself.

"Sorry," he said, "but it does feel sort of special. I suppose you must feel like that about the United States."

"I've never thought about it," Jim said, "but now that you ask me, I guess I do. It's pretty neat on the Fourth of July."

One day, when the boys were putting the finishing touches to their platform before Mr. Blair was due to inspect it, Jim Crawley said, "You're a good swimmer, eh Scott? No kidding?"

"Pretty good."

"Mr. Garfield is going to start training sessions soon. At the Y, you know. We'll have to go in the morning." Mr. Garfield was the phys-ed teacher at the school.

"So I hear."

"And then we'll have swim trials and make up teams. And the teams will go to all kinds of meets."

"I've never timed my swimming. Dan and I just did it for fun. You have to be careful in the river. You have to think of what you're doing."

"Well, I guess we'll find out how fast you are soon enough."

There was some anxiety in Jim's voice, but Scott didn't pay much attention to it.

It was fun in the treetop. The platform was a success. It was quite large, and Scott and Jim furnished it with pillows and blankets and took up picnic lunches. They often invited Tom and Greg, who laughed and called it a space platform from where they could launch ships to the stars. At times they almost believed it *was* a space ship, it was so high and free — their own version of

110

"Star Wars." If only Dan could have been there too, Scott thought, it would have been almost perfect.

Jim had seen the mask that Dan had given Scott, and one day he said, "You know that mask you have? I was thinking about it the other day. Dad knows a guy who's come to live near here who collects things like that. His name is Dr. Swanson. I think he's an archaeologist. He could tell you what it's worth."

"Worth! I don't care what it's worth," Scott said. "I'd never part with it no matter what it was worth in money." Then Scott told Jim the story of the masks. He hadn't been able to tell it before, it had been too personal, but now that he knew Jim better it was easier. "So you see why I would never, never part with it," he finished.

"Well, you never know," Jim said.

Chapter 14

Adventure and Heartache

Mrs. Blair had spoken to a well-known art instructor who had agreed to give Scott lessons after he had seen his work. Mr. Steiner, who had a very thick, curly, black beard, worked in a large studio with a sloping glass roof, filled with half-painted pictures, plaster-casts, and some fine finished pieces of art.

Scott and Mr. Steiner got on well. Mr. Steiner had a lot of unusual ideas, and his own work was startlingly original, but he thought that Scott should have a good grounding in general art to begin with. So, side by side with his creative work, Scott began to learn basics and disciplines.

"If you work hard, you could become a good painter, perhaps even a great one," his teacher told him. "Your wood work is good too. One day you might want to give up one to spend all your time on the other, but you don't have to make any decisions like that for a few years yet." And Mr. Steiner laughed heartily.

Scott knew that he needed the lessons and tried to work hard. Week after week he went to his art classes, but somehow his work was just adequate, nothing more. Sadly at first, then with more and more conviction, Scott realized that the magic and joy had gone out of painting and wood carving. It had nothing to do with Mr. Steiner or the lessons. It was simply that Scott's heart wasn't in it any more.

How badly he'd wanted oil paints when he hadn't been able to afford them! And now that he had all the paints he wanted, he had lost all interest in using them. It was hard to understand.

Painting had been so much fun in those green-forest days when Scott had sketched by the river, with Dan scrabbling his toes in the sand beside him. And whittling away at a piece of wood had seemed the natural thing to do on a snowy winter evening with Jake reading the newspaper beside the fire. But now things were different. Where had the magic gone?

Perhaps it had to do with the heartache that never left him, the heartache that he was trying to ignore. When he was doing things with his new friends, especially Jim Crawley, he could forget for a little while. But art, with its mysterious way of drawing out his innermost feelings, reminded Scott too much of home. So he had closed his heart against it.

At home, Mrs. Blair — Aunt Amelia as Scott tried to remember to call her — made new rules about homework and about Scott keeping his bedroom and the rec room tidy. Scott had never worried about his room at Twin Rivers. So long as it was clean, and he didn't fall over his stuff, it was good enough. But then he had never had so much stuff. In his new home all kinds of things were suddenly necessary, things that all the other kids around had, records and magazines and models of cars and boats, and skis and skiing equipment for the coming winter. It was hard to keep track of it all and harder still to keep it all in place.

In the meantime, the swim program at the Y had started. Mr. Garfield had begun to assess the boys and girls at the school for possible team material. Everyone was talking about it. Those who knew they had a chance

113

to get on the team started practising. Scott hoped he would make the team. It would be great to be on the same team with Jim.

Mr. Garfield had spoken both to Scott and Jim after watching them at one of their work-outs. "Both you boys have a good chance to make it for the team. But you have to work hard. I'll give you all the training you can take, but you have to be there at the right time. And that's early in the morning."

And early it was. Six o'clock found Scott and Jim cycling to the Y for their sessions. "You've got lots of things to learn," Mr. Garfield said to Scott one day, "but you could turn out to be a winner." How important was it to be a winner, Scott wondered. But the thought was flattering.

Through the fine autumn days, Scott and Jim continued to spend time together. One day they climbed Old Grimface. This was the boys' name for a forbidding rock that towered into the air, almost bare of trees, in an otherwise wooded picnic area. Old Grimface looked strangely out of place among the green-clad slopes.

"None of the boys has ever climbed it," Jim said, "but you know so much about climbing, maybe we could do it together."

"Hasn't *anyone* ever climbed it?"

"Sure. But there've been accidents. Most of the parents of the guys I know won't let them try it."

"What about your parents?"

Jim shrugged. "They've never actually said anything."

So one Saturday, with sandwiches and thermoses in backpacks, Scott and Jim went off on their bikes, as they often did. Jim had brought a rope for the climb.

They got to Old Grimface and started their climb,

Scott taking the lead. They were doing well, and were more than halfway up the scar-faced old rock, when Scott noticed that the rope that tied them together was fraying. At the same time Jim slipped.

"Hang on," Scott called to him. "Be careful, the rope's fraying."

"I can't," Jim cried, desperately, his hands clawing at an outjutting shelf, while his feet dangled below him.

"Take your weight off the rope; hold onto something; put your legs against the cliff," Scott shouted.

Somehow Jim found a foothold and clung to the face of the rock.

"Help!" Jim yelled. "Help!" His voice echoed over the woods below.

"Don't panic," Scott called. "I'll get down and give you a hand. Just hang on."

But Jim yelled again, "Help!" A group of picnickers heard his cries and came running to the scene.

Meantime, Scott was carefully working his way down and had managed to reach a shelf just above Jim. Loosened by his descent, rocks slid and rumbled away down the side of the cliff. At last Scott found a good hold on the ledge.

"I'll get you up," he panted.

"I'm too heavy for you," Jim cried. "I might pull you over."

Scott pulled the rope up past the bad bit. "We'll have to go easy. Try not to jerk. There might be another weak spot." Scott braced himself against the cliff wall and started to haul.

As Scott pulled on the rope, Jim worked his feet slowly up the side of the cliff. More rocks fell away, clattering to the ground far below. "Come on, Jim," Scott urged. "Come on."

It seemed to take forever. But Jim at last managed to get a surer hold on the ledge. "Okay," he puffed, "I think I can make it now." With Scott pulling steadily on the rope, Jim scrambled on to the ledge. There he huddled, pressed against the wall. Some of the rock had fallen away directly below them. The boys were trapped.

But the picnickers, who had been shouting encouragement from below, had also called for help. As the boys clung to their ledges, the rescue squad arrived.

"Scott," Mrs. Blair said later, sadly, "you've been doing some pretty wild and woolly things lately. Have you always done things like that?"

"Dan and I did lots of stuff," Scott said gruffly. He had been scared cold up on Old Grimface.

"I'm sort of disappointed," Mrs. Blair said.

"You didn't say I couldn't go," Scott said.

"You should have known better," she replied.

Mr. Blair said, "It was plucky of you to help Jim out the way you did. You more than likely saved his life. But it wasn't sensible, the whole thing, was it?"

That night Scott cried a little. He couldn't tell them about the nagging misery he was trying to shut out.

Scott and Jim had their allowances stopped for a few weeks so they couldn't go to shows or the skating rink. The skiing expedition they had been promised was cancelled. Jim, bored and restless, had yet another idea.

"There's nothing to do. My folks are going away for the weekend and there'll be only Mrs. Marsh at the house. Let's take Dad's boat out on the lake."

"By ourselves?" Scott looked awed.

"Why not?" Jim said. "Dad's let me take it out before."

"But not without him."

"Well, he was in the boat, but I did everything myself. I know as much about the boat as he does."

"Mrs. Marsh wouldn't like it." Mrs. Marsh was the Crawley's housekeeper.

"She goes out shopping and then to lunch with her sister Saturdays. She doesn't get back for ages. Come on, Scott."

"Well." Scott wasn't too sure, but surely there was no harm in it if they stayed close to shore. "If you think it'll be all right, it's okay with me."

"Good." Jim was pleased, and Scott was glad he'd agreed.

On Saturday morning, as soon as Mrs. Marsh left for the shopping centre, the boys lost no time. The boat was moored at a dock just by the Crawley's house. Scott and Jim were in it almost before Mrs. Marsh's car was out of sight.

There was no difficulty starting up the engine or nosing the boat slowly out into the lake. Gradually Jim opened the throttle, and soon they were speeding across the water. Jim perched up on the seat in front of the controls, and Scott stood beside him. The water churned in their wake. The boys were too thrilled to notice the clouds stealing up.

"Shall we go through the locks? We could go through to the sea," Jim Crawley suggested.

Scott didn't reply. He didn't know what to say, for he knew that this was a truly foolish thing to do. Suddenly he noticed the clouds. The wind had come up. So Scott said, "No, Jim, I think we should stay in the lake."

"Think we'll be pressing our luck?" Jim said.

Scott felt uncomfortable, but the matter was all at once taken out of his hands.

The engine coughed once or twice. The boat began to falter and bucked a few times. Then the engine stopped.

"What's happened? What's gone wrong?" Scott cried.

Jim pressed the starter over and over again. The engine did not respond. The boat was already beginning to rock in the rising wind.

118

"Oh, darn it," Jim cried, frustrated. "Oh blast! What's wrong with this old stink-pot?"

Scott examined the control panel. "Jim," he said flatly, "we've run out of gas."

"No!" Jim stared at the fuel gauge, realizing that Scott was right, that he had been in too much of a hurry to check it before they left.

The boys looked at each other in silence. The wind sang in their ears; it was already whipping up the waves. Suddenly they realized that most of the other boats had made for shelter. They were alone.

"Dad must have an emergency can of gas on board," Jim said. But they could not find it.

"He took it out to fill it up," Jim remembered, his face wretched. "We had to use it last week, and Dad hasn't had the boat out since."

"We have to get help," Scott said.

They waved a flag and hollered, and Scott sent out an S.O.S. on the horn—three short blasts, three long, three short. Help was some time in coming, but finally someone arrived to tow them in. They knew they were in trouble up to their eyebrows.

Scott told Mrs. Blair at once because he didn't want her to find out through someone else. Both Scott and Jim were grounded. They were forbidden to leave their houses after school.

But because they were culprits together, their friendship strengthened. At school their adventures made the rounds, becoming grossly exaggerated. Since the incident of Old Grimface, all the students thought they were heroes, particularly Scott, and now the boat escapade added to their fame. They were popular, the two most admired boys in the school. For Scott, school should have been great fun.

But it wasn't. His textbooks did not hold the same interest for him as they had in the smaller school back home, where the desks had been older and the paint patchy on the walls. Sometimes Scott remembered the old globe Miss Foster, his home-room teacher, had used, and the way she had always had to balance it on the stand because one of the screws was missing. The globe in the social studies room at his new school was large and magnificently illuminated from inside. But somehow the oceans did not look as deep on it, nor the frozen north as mysterious as they had seemed on Miss Foster's globe. Geography had lost its magic too, just as his art had done.

One night Scott thought about the map of Canada, which had always seemed so real to him. The places he knew had been brightly lit, just like the globe in the social studies room, and the mysterious unknown parts had seemed so enticing, so challenging. To Scott's dismay he found that the bright parts had become dim and the unknown ones cold and uncaring. He tried to bring to mind all those places that he knew, but somehow they didn't come alive. Scott panicked and tried to conjure up the faces of Jake and Dan and Gran, but they, too, remained shadowy and would not leave the background of memory.

He got out their letters, all of which he kept carefully in a drawer, and read them all again. But it didn't seem to help.

"What's happening to me?" he thought desperately. "Am I going to forget everything I've ever loved, everything that meant so much to me?" And he huddled under his wool blankets, feeling small and helpless.

Chapter 15

Swim Trials

What with school and his art lessons, his friendships, practising his swimming, and trying to remember all the rules Aunt Amelia laid down for him, Scott didn't have much free time. And that was the way he wanted it.

Scott found himself writing less and less to Jake and Dan but he knew that his many activities were not to blame. He only used them as an excuse. The reason he wasn't writing, besides the fact that it always hurt, was that he didn't know quite *what* to write. If he told them he was having a good time, Dan might think he was forgetting him. If, on the contrary, he told them the truth, they would all worry about him. So his letters were brief and bright and factual, and he left his thoughts and feelings unsaid.

Nevertheless, Dan was getting the idea that Scott was forgetting them. Dan's letters were always sad, so sometimes Scott would leave them unread for a day or two, while he gathered up courage to open them. Once Dan wrote: "I often feel lonely, and when it's worse than usual I take my mask down and send you a message. I tell you not to forget us. With all the new things you do and your new friends, you'll probably think this real dumb, but I still do it. I say, 'Don't forget you're my brother, Scott.' But are you, still?" And Scott thought of how he had tried to picture the faces of his friends at Twin Rivers one night and had failed.

With the magic gone out of his art and his school work, the only thing in his life that sparked his full interest were the forthcoming swim trials at the Y. Both he and Jim had qualified for the finals, and now it was a matter of constant practice. Every morning without fail they had a light snack and then cycled to the Y. There Mr. Garfield met them and they worked hard. In the beginning it had been Jim who had been the stronger swimmer. He had had many years of coaching and knew things that were new to Scott.

"I used to think I was a good swimmer," Scott confided to Tom Kelly, dolefully, "and now it seems that I know less than anyone else about swimming."

But Tom, who was shrewd, shook his head.

"Garfield is trying to make something special of you. Wait and see."

Perhaps Mr. Garfield was indeed trying to do just that, but it was hard to be criticized more than any of the other boys, and put through more dull corrective exercises and more strenuous performances than anyone else. He wondered if, on the other hand, rather than trying to make something special of him, Mr. Garfield actually didn't like him. When he and Dan had swum in the river, they never thought of things like breathing properly or wasted motions. It had been fun, pure fun, and now sometimes swimming was almost a chore. It was hard enough getting up so early in the morning without spending a whole hour being told how everything he did was wrong. In spite of it all, Scott couldn't help liking Mr. Garfield and so he tried his best. Once in a while he was even rewarded with a brief word of praise.

Sometimes, when Mr. Garfield had been giving him more attention than usual, Scott noticed that a change would come over Jim. He would look a bit sulky and would be short with Scott, and once or twice he was sarcastic. "You sure are the big attention-getter these days," he said once.

Scott looked at him wearily at the end of a hard session. "You already know most of the stuff he's teaching me. You've had coaching before."

"Yeah, right," Jim said. "I didn't grow up in a mud hole."

Afterwards he apologized to Scott. And Scott knew that Jim was anxious. He knew that although they had become good friends Jim did not want to lose his standing as the best swimmer in their age-group. He had been the best swimmer for so long now that it would be hard for him to accept a rival.

As the training progressed, Scott improved. He began to realize that what Tom said was true. Mr. Garfield's coaching was beginning to pay off. He knew he was swimming better than he ever had. In their practice sessions, when he happened to be swimming against Jim, he started to beat him sometimes.

In the last week before the swim trials they did not ride home together as usual. One morning Jim said he had promised to go to someone else's house for breakfast, and this was repeated several times. Scott rode home alone, hurt and disappointed. He didn't want to lose Jim's friendship. And he didn't want Jim to be a poor sport. He liked him and wanted to go on liking him.

Jim's attitude brought, besides hurt and disappointment, a new desire into Scott's life. A desire to win. He had never felt this in his carefree days in Lytton. He had always known that Dan was the stronger swimmer and he had never cared. But now the joy of swimming for its own sake was gone, and gone the feeling of exhilaration, of power over the strength of the water. Scott wanted to win. He wanted to win in spite of the fact that it was spoiling his friendship with Jim. And he knew *why* he wanted to win. It was Jim's reference to the mud hole. He was a stranger still, no matter how everyone tried to make him feel one of them. Scott wanted to win because he knew he didn't really belong.

It wasn't a good feeling.

It affected his school work and it affected his art lessons, neither of which had been going too well anyway. Scott gave all his energy to his swimming practices and had little left for studying. He often went after school to practise by himself. The Blairs belonged to a private club that had a pool, and Scott would go there when there were few people around and repeat over and over again all the things Mr. Garfield had drummed into him. The start, the breathing, the best use of his limbs. By the time he got home, he was exhausted.

"You're getting too tired, Scott," Mrs. Blair said to him. "You're overdoing it. Why don't you just rest for a couple of days?" But Scott couldn't leave the practising alone. Jim's taunt rang in his ears, and even though Jim had apologized, Scott knew that in his heart of hearts Jim had meant it.

One day Mr. Steiner, his art instructor, held up a picture that Scott had just finished. "You call this art?" he asked.

Scott shrugged.

"What would you do with it?" Mr. Steiner asked.

"Tear it up?" Scott suggested.

"I'm glad we agree," Mr. Steiner said, as he tore the picture across.

Then he put an arm around Scott. "Look, Scott, your heart and your interest just don't seem to be in these lessons. Your folks are just wasting their money. Don't you want these lessons?"

"It isn't that," Scott said, his voice husky with weariness and humiliation. "It's the swimming. Our trials are this weekend, and I just haven't had time for my art projects."

"Well," Mr. Steiner said, "we'll hope for better things when the trials are over."

At last the day for the trials arrived. The Y was packed with spectators. Schoolmates of the swimmers filled the bleachers with high-pitched voices, with shouts and laughter.

Mr. Garfield was giving the swimmers last-minute advice. The big moment had come. His ears battered by the yelling and the whistles from the stands and by the voice on the megaphone, Scott found himself beside Jim Crawley, poised, ready to dive in and compete in the finals.

"Don't drown, Canuck," Jim Crawley said to him. Canuck! It was all Scott needed. He could feel the adrenalin pour into his body. But there was little time to think about his feelings, for the whistle had sounded.

The swimmers dived in, and a roar went up from the watching crowd. Scott was conscious only of determination, of his body, excellently co-ordinated by Mr. Garfield's training, streaking forward. His only desire now was to win. The word 'Canuck' was still beating against his temples.

The roar of the crowd grew louder. Dimly Scott heard individual shouts of "Crawley, come on, Crawley," and "Anderson! That's it, Scott!" Then all was drowned in one enormous bellow, so that the whole building seemed to explode, and there was the edge of the pool and he was climbing out – and he had won!

Not only had he qualified for the team but he had broken a time record.

They were around him, all his friends, punching him, their arms around his wet neck. They were proud of him. He was proud of himself. He was so terribly proud, and this was a new feeling too. He had never needed to feel proud before. He had been happy just to be himself.

When he went into the changing room, Scott was suddenly face to face with Jim. They stood, looking at each other, Scott eager, expectant, Jim with that slightly mocking smile that Scott disliked. The room froze around them.

Then Jim said, "Terrific swim, Anderson," and he held out his hand.

"Thanks," Scott said. They shook hands, like strangers, and Jim left the locker room.

Anderson! Anderson! The word rang dully in Scott's head. Anderson, not Scott. Even *Canuck* would have been better if the tone were right. And that outstretched hand. Jim had done everything a loser was expected to do. He had congratulated the winner and shaken hands with him in front of everyone else, and only Scott understood the rebuke.

"He's being jolly decent about it," Tom Kelly said. "It must be awful for him."

"Why?" someone wanted to know. "He made the team too."

"But he's not the *best* any longer," Tom said.

The Blairs were delighted with Scott's performance. Aunt Amelia declared that a celebration was in order and she and Uncle James took Scott and his friends out to brunch on Sunday. Greg and Tom came, but Jim said thanks but he was busy. Scott had to work hard to hide his disappointment. He wouldn't have minded so much about Jim if Dan and Jake could have been there.

On Monday the school principal spoke to Scott. "Congratulations, Scott. You did very well indeed at the swim trials. Mr. Garfield spoke to me about you. Actually he's never had quite such a good swimmer in your age-group. Did he tell you that?" Mr. Crane laughed and patted Scott's shoulder. "I bet he didn't. He doesn't believe in swelled heads. But he wants you to have extra coaching for future meets. He thinks you might become a champion, Scott. Maybe even an international champion! You may represent your country some day, if you work hard enough. And wouldn't we be proud of you then!"

All day the principal's words rang in Scott's ears. However, when he got home, he said nothing about it to the Blairs. The words had set up a swirl of confusion in his mind.

Scott thought of them again: "You may represent your country some day." But *his* country was Canada, and that wasn't what the principal had meant. If he ever did become a great swimmer, he would want to do it for the people who were dear to him. To whom he belonged. Certainly the people who were around him now were friends, and he liked them, and in time no doubt they would meld into his life, but he knew that as far as he himself was concerned he would always be the boy from Twin Rivers, Jake's boy. He would want to swim for Jake, and for Dan and Gran.

It was the same with his art. Even though he had been doing badly lately, he knew that he could do better. If he ever became a good artist, he would want to be known as the artist from the Fraser Canyon, from Lytton.

Of course he might never become either, but one had to think of these things. And if he grew up to be just an ordinary guy, he would want more than ever to know where he belonged, and he would want to be true to that place and to the people he loved.

But his success and the admiration of his friends was like that wine Jake had let him have once, on New Year's Eve. It went to his head and made him dizzy. Scott knew he wasn't himself. When they had persuaded him to leave Twin Rivers, they had all said he could just give it a try. Of course none of them had ever expected the new experiment to be anything but a success for Scott. *He* was the only one who had doubted its outcome, who had actually thought of it as a trial. But what could he do?

Scott looked at the mask hanging on his wall and remembered Granny McKay's words: "When you need to know right from wrong, the mask will tell you."

But the mask hung silently on the wall and told him nothing.

Chapter 16

The Mask Creates a Stir

One evening Mrs. Blair had a dinner party. Among the thirty-odd guests were the Kellys and the Rolstons and the Crawleys, and another couple by the name of Swanson. Dr. and Mrs. Jonathan Swanson were newcomers to the neighborhood.

It was the first time that Mrs. Blair had given a formal dinner party since Scott had come to live with the Blairs. Mrs. Blair said that Scott could invite his special friends for the evening. Dinner would be served to them in the downstairs rec room, and they could have their own fun, providing they didn't disturb her guests upstairs. The dinner was important to her, she said. There were business friends of Mr. Blair's coming and she was anxious that everything should go off smoothly.

In the afternoon, busy-looking people came to the house with baskets of flowers. Later, the caterers arrived and began setting out elegant trays of hors d'oeuvres and preparing the dining room table for the buffet supper. Aunt Amelia looked flushed and pretty in a new blue dress — blue like the lake on a fine day, Scott thought.

The guests started to arrive soon after six, and Scott, Tom, and Greg went to the rec room where they decided to play scrabble. A little later Jim arrived. He said he had actually wanted to go to a show with someone else but his parents had made him come. Scott made no comment on this announcement. Upstairs they could hear the grown-ups talking and laughing.

"And they told *us* to be quiet," Greg said laughing.

While they were having dinner, Jim said, "You know that archaeologist fellow's here. Dr. Swanson. He wants to see your mask, Scott. I told him about it."

"Why did you do that?" Scott asked sharply.

"Because I think it's neat, and he's interested in old stuff like that."

A vague anxiety stirred in Scott. "I wish you hadn't," he said.

"Why, what harm can it do?"

Scott shrugged. He didn't have an answer for Jim. He really didn't know why he should feel uneasy. He turned on the television. "Let's watch 'Love Boat,'" he said.

It was about nine o'clock when Mrs. Blair came down to the rec room and beckoned to Scott.

"Scott, Dr. Swanson, one of our guests, is an archaeologist with the university and he'd love to see that mask of yours. Do you think you could show it to him?"

Anxiety stirred in Scott again, stronger this time. But surely there was no reason in the world why he shouldn't show his mask to an interested archaeologist. He left the boys to the television and went upstairs to get it.

In his room, Scott took the mask down from the wall and held it in his hands. He tried to conjure up the eyes in the cavities, the wise eyes he used to imagine he could see. But the cavities were blank and communicated nothing. Scott went down to the living room with his mask.

The room was alive with people, so different from its cold, withdrawn, everyday appearance. A fire was blazing in the grate, and people were sitting in little groups, talking and laughing as they sipped tea and coffee and ate little cakes.

When Mrs. Blair saw Scott, she came hurrying over to him, the lake-blue dress swirling round her legs. She drew him into the crowded living room and introduced him to a tall grey-haired man who shook hands with him gravely and then took the mask from him and examined it with interest. Others crowded round to see the wonderful mask.

"And where did you say you got it?" asked Dr. Swanson.

"A friend gave it to me, up in Lytton. It was in his family. No one knows where it came from originally," Scott explained.

"Extraordinary," said Dr. Swanson.

"An interesting piece?" Mr. Blair questioned.

"Certainly interesting," Dr. Swanson said. "If I'm not mistaken, some collector would give a lot of money for it. Or some museum. Are you in the market?" he asked Scott with a smile.

"What do you mean?" Scott asked, his throat tight.

"I mean, do you want to sell your mask?"

"Oh no," Scott cried. "No. Never. I would *never* sell it. Not for anything in the world!"

"Well, you might just change your mind when you hear what it is worth," Dr. Swanson said. "Of course what I say would have to be verified, but it seems like a pretty ancient piece to me. You might be fooling around with something very valuable, young man."

"I don't ever fool around with it," Scott protested, "and I don't care what it's worth."

"That's just what I mean," Dr. Swanson said, wagging his finger at Scott. "You don't care what it's worth. Of course you don't. You don't understand about monetary values yet. You're just a boy, and you simply enjoy the mask. But this mask is not a toy, Scott."

A weakness spread through Scott's stomach, replacing the fear. It spread to every part of his body. It was that same feeling he had had at Twin Rivers when he had been persuaded to go to Bellevue with the Blairs, a wordless despair, a helpless conviction that no matter what he felt or said, the grown-ups would have their way.

"I *know* it's not a toy," he said in a husky voice. "I've *never* thought of it as a toy. And besides, I don't play with toys any more. It's not worth anything in money to me. It's...it's..."

"It was given to him by a friend," Aunt Amelia stepped in. "It has sentimental value for Scott."

"It's even more than that," Scott said. "It's hard to explain."

The professor glanced at Mr. Blair and winked. That wink was like a stab wound to Scott. The men were laughing at him, thinking he was just a dumb kid, hanging on to the mask for some silly kid reason. He hated this cool, grey-haired archaeologist. He wished him at the bottom of Lake Washington.

"Okay," said Dr. Swanson, "suppose we just give it to a proper appraiser — that's a person who knows the value of these old things — and find out what it's worth. Just for fun."

"No," said Scott, "I don't want to do that either."

"Scott," said Aunt Amelia gently, "you're not being polite. Dr. Swanson's doing this for *you*."

133

"No, he's not," Scott burst out. His throat and his eyes burned. "He's doing it for himself—because he wants to buy my mask himself."

For a moment there was a shocked silence in the room. Then Dr. Swanson said, "Really!"

Mrs. Blair had turned quite pink. Her lips looked pinched. "You must apologize to Dr. Swanson at once, Scott," she said.

"I'm sorry if I was rude," Scott mumbled. "But I still mean what I said."

Mrs. Blair took the mask from Dr. Swanson and gave it back to Scott. "Take your mask back to your room," she said, her voice brittle as slate.

Scott, eyes stinging, made his way through the crowd of guests.

"Oh, you shouldn't be angry with him, Amelia," cried Mrs. Swanson. "It *is* his mask. He doesn't have to have it appraised. Jonathan, you were pressuring the boy. You weren't being fair."

But Mrs. Blair had turned her back on Scott, who, clutching his mask, stumbled towards the stairs.

"Scott was right," came an unexpected voice from the living-room door. The voice was Jim Crawley's. "You *would* like to buy that mask, Dr. Swanson, I know. You've been interested in seeing it ever since I told you about it."

"Jim!" gasped Mrs. Crawley.

"You said a collector might be interested. You're that collector," Jim persisted.

Dr. Swanson reddened. "I never thought Scott felt so strongly about it," he said.

"Okay, but you do know now. So just don't say you're doing it for Scott," said the unquenchable Jim. "You still want to persuade him to sell it."

There was a stir among the guests.

"I don't see anything wrong with that," Dr. Swanson said brusquely. "I'm a collector, and Scott has something valuable to sell."

"Scott hasn't got *anything* to sell," said Jim, and quickly left the room.

"What have I done to deserve that boy?" groaned Mrs. Crawley. "I do apologize for him, Amelia."

"Well, never mind," Mrs. Blair said in a desperate attempt to restore a comfortable atmosphere. "Let's have some more coffee and forget about Scott and Jim."

Upstairs in the room with the green wall-to-wall carpeting that felt like forest moss, Scott rubbed the tears from his eyes and held the mask in his damp hands. Suddenly there was a knock on his door.

"Come in," Scott said wearily.

It was Jim. Scott looked at him in surprise. "Thanks for standing up for me," he said.

"I had to say it. It was true," Jim said gruffly. "Grown-ups have a way of working around you." Then he added, "Look here, Scott, about that business at the Y. I'm sorry. I acted like an idiot."

"It's okay," Scott said.

"Can we be friends again?"

"I always hoped we could be. I've missed you."

"And have I ever missed you, Scott. Now I'm really sorry I told Swanson about your mask. I never thought it would cause all this trouble."

Scott thought for a minute, then he shook his head. "No, I'm glad you told him, Jim. You see, it made me realize something very important."

"What was that?"

"Granny was right. The mask did come through," Scott said.

"Came through?"

"Dan's Gran said it would help me when I needed it, and it did."

"What do you mean?"

"When Dr. Swanson asked if I wanted to sell the mask, I realized what was happening. He wanted me to *sell* the thing I loved most! And now I realize that that's exactly what I've been doing here all along. I've been selling myself. I've been trading my true self for things I don't need to be happy."

Jim stared at Scott in dismay.

"Do you mean to say you don't like living here?"

"I don't belong here, Jim. I belong back at Lytton with Jake."

"You're just saying that because you're mad about what happened."

"Maybe," Scott said, "but sometimes when you're mad you get to see things better."

There was another knock on the door. "Come on, you guys," Tom Kelly called. "Come on downstairs."

'We're coming," Scott replied. His voice was still thoughtful.

When the party was over and the guests gone, Scott lay in bed wide awake, his mind going round in circles. By morning he knew what he had to do. The message from the mask was clear.

He knew that he had to go back. The question was how? If he spoke of it to the Blairs, they would just say that he was a bit upset and would get over it. They would say he hadn't given the trial enough time. If he wrote to Jake, Jake would tell him to think about it a little longer.

Whatever he did, he would have to do by himself.

He would need money for the trip. The Blairs gave him an allowance, but he did not want to take any of their money when he was going to leave them. When he had the opportunity, he phoned and found that the bus fare to Vancouver was $15.60. That was as far as he needed to go. In Vancouver, Sandy Black would help him. Sandy had understood the way Scott felt. He should have a little more money than that in case of emergency. He would have to sell his rock collection.

Scott knew a boy at school who had offered to trade a radio with a digital clock for Scott's collection. Perhaps Ricky Gordon would consider a cash deal.

The next day Scott packed his rocks and set out for Ricky's house.

Ricky Gordon considered the cash deal. "I don't have that much cash," he said. "Maybe Mr. Mackenzie will give us something for my radio. Let's go there tomorrow after school."

Mr. Mackenzie had a store that was like a flea market. It was full of miscellaneous objects. He turned the radio around in his hands, clicked it on and off, and offered Ricky ten dollars for it.

"Ten dollars!" Scott groaned. "But the man at the rock store said my collection was worth twenty-five."

"Maybe my mom will give me an advance on my allowance," Ricky said. "Let's go ask her."

At Ricky's home, Mrs. Gordon examined the collection. "Why are you selling it?" she asked Scott.

Scott's heart sank. Mrs. Gordon didn't know Aunt Amelia, but things got around. He stood tongue-tied.

"It's Christmas, isn't it?" Mrs. Gordon offered brightly. "Of course, I understand. You'll be needing money for presents pretty soon. All right, I'll advance the money, Ricky. I'll advance you ten dollars."

"Will that be okay?" Ricky asked eagerly.

"Sure, okay," Scott said.

Chapter 17

North-Bound Express

It was early December and it had turned cold. Mrs. Blair had bought Scott a new winter jacket, even though he had protested and had said that the one he'd brought with him from Twin Rivers was still good enough. Jake had only bought it the previous year. So Mrs. Blair had made Scott try it on — and had laughed at him. It was now too short, and his hands and wrists stuck out of the sleeves, like potato sprouts, Mrs. Blair said. But now he'd have to leave the new jacket behind — he didn't want to take anything that the Blairs had bought.

Scott planned his departure. Every Monday Aunt Amelia went to downtown Seattle to shop and have lunch with her friends. She never got back much before supper, and on Mondays they always had cold cuts and potato salad. Monday would be the obvious day.

Scott's choice fell on the very next Monday. There was no point in delay. He went to school in the morning, and it was the longest morning of his life. It was difficult to keep his secret, but he knew that a word dropped carelessly might upset all his plans. At noon he hurried home, and, first of all, even before eating his lunch, he ran up to Mr. Blair's study.

Scott had to find his Canadian papers. He couldn't relax until he had them in his hands. His whole plan depended on them. Without them he couldn't possibly get across the border back into Canada.

Dimly he remembered Uncle James putting the papers in his desk. Uncle James had taken him on a grand tour of the house the night he had arrived, and, in his study, he had removed Scott's papers from his breast-pocket and placed them carefully in one of the drawers of his desk. Scott did not like going into Uncle James' desk, but he simply had to have his papers.

In spite of the fact that the house was empty, Scott entered the darkly panelled room on tiptoe. The rows of books along the walls, the deep leather chairs, the huge, polished desk, all seemed to eye him disapprovingly.

"I won't touch anything else," he whispered as though they could hear him. "I'll take only what belongs to me."

Carefully Scott opened the drawer in which Uncle James had put the papers. They were still there! In fact they looked as though they had never been touched. Scott lifted them out. He could feel his heart hammering against his ribs with the joy of having the papers in his hands. He shut the drawer softly and started to leave the room.

At the door he turned for a moment. He could smell the leather and the polish and the faint, musty odor of books. This was Mr. Blair's room, and Scott would miss him. Maybe he was ungrateful to be leaving this home and this heritage. But it was not *his* heritage.

"I'm sorry," Scott whispered. "I don't like doing it this way."

139

Then he ran down to the kitchen for his lunch of sandwiches and fruit, carefully prepared for him by Aunt Amelia and left in the fridge. As soon as he had finished, he hurried up to his room.

He had to make sure that he wasn't taking anything with him that belonged to the Blairs or anything that they had bought him. A few days before, he had rummaged in his cupboard until he found the very clothes he had worn when he had left Twin Rivers. Now he took off what he was wearing and put on the old clothes. Good heavens, he sure had grown! But they would have to do. He loosened his belt so that the trousers barely sat on his hips. In this way they nearly reached his ankles. The shirt was tight and short in the sleeves, but no one would see it under his jacket. He got out that jacket, the one Aunt Amelia had laughed at, and Scott had to admit that it did look funny. He tried to pull the sleeves down, but was warned by an ominous ripping sound not to pull any harder. Oh well, the sleeves would just have to be short. Quickly Scott packed his suitcase with only those things he had brought with him from Twin Rivers. He looked with longing at the many lovely things the Blairs had bought him — the books, the car models, the sporting equipment, the records — but somehow none of this seemed to belong to him.

At the very last, Scott went into the cupboard and brought out the picture that he had removed from the wall so that he could hang up his mask. Aunt Amelia never had hung it anywhere else after all. Carefully Scott took down the mask and replaced the picture. He wrapped the mask in one of his shirts and added it to his few possessions, already in the suitcase. Gently Scott closed the lid. The locks snapped loudly in the quiet room.

The night before he had written a little note to the Blairs: "Dear Aunt Amelia and Uncle James, Please don't think me rotten or ungrateful. I'm really and truly grateful for what you tried to do for me, but it just isn't working. I can't stay any longer. I can't forget Jake and Dan and Gran, because they're my family. Thank you for everything, but I have to go back."

As he reread the note, Scott felt terrible. He had grown fond of Aunt Amelia and Uncle James. He thought of all the good times he had had with them, the sailing and Aunt Amelia's shopping sprees, and the way Uncle James had helped him and his friends with the tree platform, and of the lunch up on the Space Needle when Uncle James had said so hopefully, "It's not going too badly, is it?" Scott even thought fondly of Aunt Amelia's rules, and of how proud she had been when he had done so well at the swim trials.

But he knew that none of this could make up for the sense of loss that never left him. However, he got his pen and added a postscript to the note: "Please don't think I don't love you. I do, very much. And I hope you will come to visit sometimes." Then, with a shrinking heart, he propped the note up against the fruit dish on the smooth, white kitchen table. As he did this, he thought of Granny McKay's well-worn table-top, with the mugs of cocoa and his favorite almond cookies. How good it was going to be to get back to all that again.

With everything done, Scott picked up the suitcase and hurried out of the house. He hoped none of the neighbors would see him, for he certainly looked very odd in his old clothes. It was a fair distance to the bus stop, and Scott slipped through the lane and onto a street where hardly anyone would know him. Soon he had boarded a bus that would take him to the bus depot.

141

The depot was crowded, and Scott felt small and nervous. But nobody took the slightest notice of him. Busy, important-looking people strode by him with heavy bags and looked straight ahead.

It was no use standing about, wasting time. Scott might as well gather up his courage and find out what he was supposed to do. He would have to buy his ticket, but which was the right wicket? What if he bought the wrong ticket? There was another Vancouver, near Portland.

"Come on, young 'un, don't stand in the way. Are you lost or something?" asked a burly man with a huge bag in his right hand, and a cage with a canary in his left.

"I want to buy a ticket for Vancouver," Scott said. "Vancouver, British Columbia."

"Well, don't dither around, that's the line right in front of you. Can't you read? It says 'Vancouver,' doesn't it? Open your eyes; must always keep your eyes open in this life," and the man pushed off, shouting at all and sundry to make way for him. Yes, the sign on the wicket did say "Vancouver."

Scott joined the line and bought his ticket. He put the change carefully in his pocket. That money was all he had, and he mustn't lose it.

Then he followed a large woman who was also going to Vancouver. She wasn't frightened of anyone and spoke in a haughty voice to the driver, asking him if she were boarding the right bus and if she could trust the porter with her luggage.

"There's a sign on the bus, ma'am," the bus driver said patiently.

"Oh well, you can't be careful enough," the woman said huffily.

But Scott was glad she had asked, for it had saved him from having to ask and feeling silly.

Scott's ticket was punched, and he climbed into the bus. He took a seat by the window and chose to put his suitcase at his feet rather than up on the rack in case someone took it by mistake. He didn't care that much about his few pieces of clothing, but his mask was in it.

Scott felt as if the bus would never start. Suppose someone had seen him leaving and had got in touch with Uncle James. Scott knew that if the Blairs came to take him off the bus it would be a long time before he'd be able to gather up enough courage to do this again. But at last the bus started up and began to move out of the depot. Scott breathed more easily.

Soon they were speeding through a dismal, grey countryside. The sky looked stormy, as though it might, at any moment, part with its burden of snow. Twin Rivers, Scott thought, would be under snow, the rivers steely, the fire in Jake's parlor roaring up the chimney. Then another thought hit Scott, and sweat broke out all over him. If Aunt Amelia happened to come home early and see his note, the Blairs might phone to the border and have him stopped there!

Why had he been so silly as to leave that note? He should have waited until he was safely home and then sent the Blairs a telegram. Of course if anyone questioned him, he would tell them that he was going home, that he still belonged to Jake O'Burn, but he knew that it wouldn't be any use. They would talk to him, patiently and kindly, and make him do as they wanted, in the way of all grown-ups.

The journey to the border seemed endless, even though the bus was an express. Would they never get to Blaine? Scott could have enjoyed watching the grey countryside whizz by if he hadn't been so afraid of what might be waiting for him at the border.

143

At last a sign announced that they were passing Blaine, and a few moments after that the bus rumbled past the Peace Arch and stopped. Immigration and Customs officers appeared. The luggage was hauled out for Customs inspection. The passengers filed out. In a minute Scott was standing in front of a friendly officer, who was smiling down at him.

"And where are you going, young fellow?" the officer asked.

"Home," Scott said, and added "to Lytton."

"Are you alone?"

"Yes."

The man frowned a little and Scott's heart beat faster.

"Canadian?"

Scott nodded.

"May I see your papers?"

"Scott handed them over. The officer looked at the papers and nodded to himself.

"Born in Canada, eh? How long have you been in the States?"

"About four months. I was visiting."

"Bringing anything over?"

Scott shook his head. Scott opened his suitcase for the Customs inspection.

"What's this we have here?" The officer had taken Scott's mask out of its wrapping and was looking at it. Scott's heart froze.

"It's my mask."

"Did you buy this in the States?"

"No, I didn't. My friend at home gave it to me before I left. Up in Lytton."

"It looks like something that should be in a museum," the officer said.

"It's mine," Scott said. He couldn't stop his lip from trembling, so he held it between his teeth. "You could ask my guardian, Jake O'Burn, up in the canyon," he added.

The officer shrugged. "I don't think we'll need to do that. Take care of it; looks like it's valuable." With a smile he handed the mask back to Scott and gave his attention to the next passenger.

Scott could hardly hide his relief. But he was still anxious. If Uncle James was going to have him stopped, now would be the time.

"Oh please hurry, hurry," he silently begged the Customs officials. But they took their time, and Scott, back in the bus now, had to wait.

But at last the officials were finished, the luggage piled back in the bus, the doors slammed. The bus started up with a roar. They were on their way.

"Home, I'm *home*," Scott whispered to himself. All at once the lights came on again on the map of Canada he carried inside him and Scott felt the warm, happy glow that he hadn't had since he'd left Twin Rivers.

He could relax on the ride to Vancouver. Nobody could stop him now, for he was home in Canada, and he was still Jake O'Burn's boy.

Chapter 18

The Frightening Message

It was dark when the bus roared into the Vancouver depot, and Scott was hungry. Snow was just beginning to fall, but that didn't matter. Nothing mattered, for he was home in Canada. Scott slipped into the cafeteria and ordered a hamburger. He didn't have much money left when he had finished eating.

Scott looked up Sandy Black's address in the phone book and then asked directions. The girl behind the wicket looked at him curiously as she gave him the information. He was to get the bus for West Vancouver on Georgia Street, at the corner of Homer. He would get a transfer for another bus at Park Royal.

Scott walked out into the cold, grey snow-bespattered evening. Everywhere the lights were lit, and people hurried by with their collars turned up and scarves wrapped round their necks. The wind blew through Scott's thin pant-legs. He was wearing summer trousers.

Scott watched carefully to be sure he got on the right bus. He couldn't afford to make a mistake and have to pay another fare. At last the bus came, Scott climbed on, and again asked for directions.

The bus driver smiled at Scott, gave him a transfer and said, "Sit up front and I'll tell you when to get off."

The bus swayed and jolted, but to Scott it was heaven. He was warm and fed now, and his happiness crept up into his chest like a big bubble. He couldn't wait to see Dan's face. And Granny McKay, how she would hug him! He couldn't even think of Jake, for the bubble was very close to bursting and at that point he might just cry a bit. He didn't plan to do that.

Nothing could go wrong now.

Scott couldn't see much out of the window because the lights in the bus were making reflections and the snow was now falling quite heavily. At last the bus driver called to Scott that the next stop was his. Scott got off to wait for his next bus.

How cold it was! But Scott was lucky—the bus he needed arrived in a few moments. This trip was shorter. Still, it was after eight when he got off the bus. At last he was on the last lap of his journey to Sandy Black's house.

Although Scott felt that he knew it so well, he had some difficulty finding the street. Everything looked so different in the dark and through the snow. Scott walked quickly down one street, but found himself in a strange neighborhood. Finally he had to knock on a door and ask for directions. Even that did not upset him, the feeling of being safe at home was so strong.

There was the house at last, just as he'd seen it in the summer, except that the garden was empty of flowers and covered with snow. There was a light in the window, and Scott could see Sandy with his feet up reading a magazine. He ran up the steps and rang the bell.

Never had there been a person more astonished than Sandy Black when he saw the funny figure in the short pants and the tight coat, powdered with snow, standing in his doorway.

The light from the hallway fell on the bright hair, glistening with snowflakes.

"Well, bless my boots!" gasped Sandy Black.

But the face under the damp hair, although red with cold, was radiant.

"Sandy!" Scott cried, "I'm home!"

"I'm home!" he repeated to Mrs. Black, who had joined her husband and was staring at Scott open-mouthed. But she was more practical than Sandy and recovered quickly.

"Take those wet things off right away," she said, "and run him a hot bath, Sandy. He'll catch his death. Where on earth have you come from, Scott? I thought you were in Seattle."

"I was," Scott said, "but I'm going back to Twin Rivers. To Jake. Oh, Sandy, Mrs. Black, I couldn't, just *couldn't*, stay there. I couldn't be without Jake and Dan and Gran and the river."

Mrs. Black and Sandy exchanged looks, but Scott was too excited to see the expression on their faces.

When he had had a steaming bath, they let him talk, and all those months of pent-up homesickness came pouring out of him. Scott sat drinking hot milk and eating oatmeal cookies in Sandy Black's bathrobe, feeling as though he was just waking up after a long, confusing dream. But just as he finished telling the Blacks about coming across the border, he became aware that Sandy and Katy were looking strangely upset.

Scott stopped talking and looked at them question-ingly, fear tugging at him.

"What's the matter?" he asked.

"Scott," Sandy said, putting his big hand on Scott's smaller one, "I have bad news for you. Jake may not be at Twin Rivers any more, nor Dan, nor Annie McKay."

"What do you mean?" Scott's heart started to hammer.

"You see, when you left, Jake couldn't stand living there without you, and just a few days ago I got a letter from him saying that he'd decided to go north — that he was selling the motel and leaving Twin Rivers — and he thought he might take Dan and Annie McKay with him. So Jake may not be there, if he's managed to sell the place. He said one party was interested, but I haven't heard anything more."

Scott's heart seemed to stop. This was what the mask had been telling him — oh, what could he do?

Suddenly Scott jumped to his feet.

"Sandy, we have to go right away — you and I — don't you see, we have to stop Jake from going. Oh, Sandy, please, please take me to Twin Rivers. I can't go back to the Blairs — I can't. I have to find Jake."

"Scott! The canyon roads are dangerous in this weather. And at night! How can you ask . . . ?" Katy Black began, but Sandy was already on his feet.

"Nothing is dangerous when I handle it," he declared. "Of course I'll take you if it's necessary. But it may not be. Let's try phoning first. Let's not panic."

Long Distance had a great deal of trouble reaching Twin Rivers. It seemed that there had been storms, and the lines had been damaged. While Sandy drank coffee, smoked a long cigar, and tapped his fingers on the table, Mrs. Black asked Scott an endless stream of questions about the Blairs, their home, and how they lived. At last the phone rang. Twin Rivers had been reached. In a few moments there was a voice on the line, a tired, cracked voice. It was old Jeremiah.

"Jeremiah, it's Sandy Black here," Sandy shouted into the mouthpiece. "Where's Jake?"

Scott held his breath while Jeremiah was answering.

"When? When did he go?" Sandy asked, and Scott felt a deep, stabbing fear.

"Where in Kamloops? Do you know where he's staying? What? Well, do you know the name of the real estate office? Try, Jeremiah. Try! It's really important. I'll explain when I write. I've got to get Jake before he sells the motel. What? Lake? Lake what?"

Sandy tapped his fingers on the kitchen table in impatience and despair.

"Was it Lakeside? Lakeside Realty? It was? You're sure, eh? Okay, Jeremiah, thanks. Thanks awfully. I'll let you know the whole story later."

Sandy banged down the receiver. "I didn't tell Jeremiah you were here, Scott. I didn't want to upset him and get him rattled." Then Sandy dialled Long Distance again.

"I want to get in touch with Lakeside Realty in Kamloops. No, I don't know the address."

There was another long wait, during which Sandy explained the situation to Scott and Katy.

"Jake's gone to Kamloops to sign the papers in the morning for the sale of Twin Rivers. Jeremiah doesn't know where he's staying, but he remembered the real estate agents — Lakeside Realty. Maybe there's still someone in the office, like a janitor or something, and I could get the name of one of the partners. The phone's ringing now."

They all waited in breathless silence as second after second ticked by.

At last Sandy said, "All right, Operator. No, I suppose there's no one there. No, don't bother." He hung up.

"No one there," he said. "Jake will probably sign the

papers first thing in the morning. We've got to get there and prevent him." He turned to Scott. "We'll have to drive there ourselves, Scotty-boy."

Katy Black protested. "In such weather! There's been nothing but storms in the Canyon. Why can't we phone the office in the morning—first thing—at nine o'clock? Or Jeremiah? Couldn't he go?"

"Jeremiah is far too old to travel through the snow. No, we can't leave it to him. And phoning the office in the morning would be too much of a risk. There are several partners. By the time somebody figured out what I wanted, Twin Rivers could have been sold. We can't risk that."

"But Sandy. . ." Katy started to protest. But she knew only too well that there was nothing Sandy liked better than a challenge.

"No buts about it," he said. "Let's get the kid's clothes dry. It takes about five or six hours driving to Kamloops, but with the snow and possible delays it might take a bit longer. I'll have a bit of shut-eye, and we'll get going before midnight. We'll be at Lakeside Realty when they open their doors in the morning."

"I'll pack a lunch for you," Katy said, knowing it was useless to protest any more. "And what about the Blairs? They'll be sick with worry."

"No, no, I left them a note," Scott reassured her.

"But we should let them know you're here. We must phone them."

"Oh no," Scott protested. "I don't want to talk to them. Not just yet, *please*."

And Katy Black understood. "All right," she agreed. "I'll take care of it myself."

Chapter 19

A Race with Time

It was snowing heavily when they got into Sandy's station wagon. Mrs. Black handed them their lunch and a flask of coffee.

"Good luck," she smiled, but Scott could see that her eyes were anxious. Was he doing a terrible thing taking Sandy out on a night like this?

"Don't worry, Katy," Sandy said, as if reading their thoughts. "I know the canyon road like the back of my hand, and I'll drive carefully. We'll get there all right. I'll phone."

The station wagon started up, and the wheels crunched through the snow. Scott sat stiffly upright. He felt sick with worry again.

If they didn't get through the canyon to Kamloops in time and Twin Rivers was sold, Jake would, without doubt, send Scott back to the Blairs. For what could Jake do with a youngster like Scott somewhere up north when he wasn't too sure what he himself would be doing?

The roads were skiddy and the going slow. However, once they left Vancouver the snow eased, and after an hour or so the stars dared to peer out among the still-threatening clouds. At Hope, they crossed the Fraser River and started along the canyon road. How mysterious were the mountainsides, how beautiful the pines and cedars and the trim firs with their mantles of snow.

The curving highway slipped away, section by section by section. Sandy spoke little, but sat, alert and determined, concentrating on his driving. The motion and the warmth of the car soon proved too much for Scott, in spite of his anxiety, and he dropped off to sleep. At Boston Bar the car was stopped by a road crew with flashlights.

"Snowslide just ahead," the flag-man said to Sandy. "The snowplows will be coming up, but it'll be a while. You could go back to that little place, just off the highway —Joe's Hamburgers. There are a few others there." He laughed. "Might get kind of crowded soon. Better get yourselves a place."

"How long will it take to clear the highway?" asked Sandy, as Scott, who had wakened as soon as the station wagon had stopped, peered out of the window, trying to see something in the dark.

"Take a few hours," the flag-man said."This is a pretty big slide."

"Sandy," Scott cried, gripping Sandy's arm, "isn't there another way? Can't we get through somehow? Maybe we could get to Jeremiah and have him drive us in his jeep. Or maybe he could go? Can't we phone or something?"

"There's no other way, Scott," Sandy said. "But all right, we'll try phoning Jeremiah. Maybe he'll be able to get through somehow, although I sure hate to send an oldster like that out into this snow."

153

But when they got to the restaurant, they discovered that the phone lines were down with the slide and all communication with the rest of the world had been cut off. Scott's face was twisted with the effort of holding back tears of disappointment.

"I'm sorry, Scotty," Sandy said. "There's nothing we can do. We can only wait and hope and keep our fingers crossed."

In the bleakness of that moment, Scott realized that just waiting was sometimes the only thing left to do. And Sandy was being so helpful and understanding and patient, he'd be only hurting him by constant complaining. So Scott sat down wearily beside Sandy.

In the booth, which Scott and Sandy were sharing with three other people, Scott fell asleep again, his head pillowed against Sandy's shoulder. From time to time, he half wakened, dimly aware that someone had produced cards and that the little roadside restaurant was full of smoke and talk and laughter and the smell of French fries. Asleep again, Scott dreamed that he was back at Twin Rivers and that Joe Fricton and Sammy Gore and Pete Boggle were playing cards with Jake.

Then suddenly someone was shaking him gently. It was Sandy.

"Come on, Scotty-boy. The road's clear. We'll have to hurry."

As they ran to the station wagon, pulling on their jackets, the sun was rising. The magnificent canyon sang in the early-morning light, a song of glittering ice and snow and steely waters, but Scott had no time to listen to the grand familiar song, for Sandy was already starting the engine. Almost before Scott had closed his door and buckled on his seat-belt, Sandy had swung out onto the highway.

"Make sure that belt's fastened properly and hang on for dear life," Sandy said, as the station wagon purred effortlessly over the newly-cleared road. "We'll have to make this trip in double-quick time."

The road flashed by, mountainside on the right, canyon on the left, wide-flung in wintry splendor, but Scott's eyes were glued to the little clock on the dashboard. They passed Lytton. Somewhere among the trees was Twin Rivers. In his house Dan would be sleeping, probably dreaming troubled dreams about the sale of Twin Rivers. They reached the Thompson River and sped along its lofty bank.

"Hurry, Sandy, hurry," Scott begged. At Spence's Bridge they crossed to the opposite bank of the river. Ashcroft, Cache Creek, the names whizzed by. It was nearly half past eight.

"It's over seventy kilometres yet," Scott cried. "We'll never make it by nine, Sandy."

Sandy didn't answer. Scott watched the speedometer climb slowly. Sandy's face was set, but at nine o'clock they were still sixteen kilometres from Kamloops.

Scott sagged with disappointment and sat staring hopelessly out of the window as the car finally left the highway to enter the city of Kamloops. Sandy slackened speed, down, down, to a bare fifty kilometres an hour. Scott watched the houses and the shops crawl by.

All at once he leapt straight up, every nerve in his body on fire. There, just entering a door, was a well-remembered, dearly-loved figure, a little more bent, smaller in the strange city street than on the porch at Twin Rivers, but unmistakable.

"Jake!" Scott yelled. At the same moment Sandy braked and pulled to the curb, right at the door of Lakeside Realty.

Flicking off his safety belt and throwing open the car door, Scott leapt out onto the pavement and threw himself at Jake.

How good that sandpapery cheek felt, how safe those arms. And Scott didn't have to explain anything, for Sandy was doing it for him.

All at the same time, Jake's face revealed astonishment, joy, and confusion.

"But what about the poor Blairs?" he asked at last. "They'll be dreadfully worried. They'll probably have the whole police force out looking for you, Scott."

"No, no, I left them a note, and Mrs. Black phoned them," Scott assured him. "They'll understand."

"They'll be furious, more likely," Jake declared. He held Scott at arm's length. "You've got a screw loose somewhere in that head of yours, Scotty-boy." Then he put his arms around Scott again. "But it's sure good to see you."

"You won't send me back, will you, Jake?" Scott asked beseechingly.

"No, I won't send you back," Jake said, shaking his head.

Jake went into Lakeside Realty and apologized for his change in plans. Something quite unexpected had come up, he said. He was beaming with such obvious delight that no one could have been annoyed with him. Scott wanted to phone Dan, but the lines were still down.

So they all three went to a pancake house, where Scott and Sandy had breakfast, consuming astonishing quantities of hot cakes, eggs, and bacon. Then they got into the station wagon and drove to Twin Rivers. This time the glittering song of the ice and snow and the lakes and the grey river came through loud and clear to Scott, and he smiled quietly. For the first time in many months his heart was singing too.

As Scott had known, Dan was heart-broken at having to leave Twin Rivers. That morning, he was huddled in a corner by the fire in his grandmother's house, trying to read, when all at once he stirred and looked out of the window. The snow had stopped falling, and a trillion diamonds had appeared outside the house, but Dan didn't pay any attention to them. He was having that daydream again. Something was going to happen. By some magic Scott was going to return.

Dan sat, as in a spell, waiting, holding on to the dream. He had had it often before, and it had always failed him.

Then Dan was sure he heard car doors slamming, the sound of voices and laughter, and the barking of a dog. That was Flappy, old Flappy who had to be given away soon. The voices came nearer, mixed now with the tramping of feet on hard snow, nearer and louder. Still Dan did not move, for he thought he was dreaming, and one false move would shatter the dream. But when the voices were right at the door, the pounding of fists was shaking the house, the heavy feet were still stamping, knocking snow off large boots, Dan sprang up and flew to the door.

And there they were, Sandy and Jake and *Scott*. Dan couldn't believe what he was seeing.

"It's my dream," he kept repeating. "I know it's my dream. I've dreamt this so many times — that you've come back, Scott. I *must* still be dreaming."

"No, you're not, silly," Scott cried, and pinched Dan so hard that he yelled in pain.

Then everyone shouted with laughter, while Flappy ran round and round, yelping hysterically.